A MAJORITY OF ONE

"I need some help," I confided. I gestured to one of the empty stone benches which lined the small park adjacent to the building. "Why don't we sit?"

"You need some help," Detective Rothwax mused. "And I thought the Cat Woman always worked alone."

But he followed me to the bench and sat listening without any further teasing or jokes. I outlined the events leading to the "suicide"—the peppermint tea party, the last few moments I had spent with Barbara, the scream, the realization that the speck on the road below was my friend—everything up to and including the conclusions I had drawn about Barbara's death.

Having heard me out, Rothwax was staring down at his nails. "Let me just ask you this," Rothwax said. "Is there one single other person who was at the peppermint party who thinks she was murdered?"

"No," (and I know I hissed), "of course not. Only me."

A
Cat by Any
Other Name

An Alice Nestleton Mystery

by
Lydia Adamson

A SIGNET BOOK

SIGNET
Published by the Penguin Group
Penguin Books USA Inc., 375 Hudson Street,
New York, New York 10014, U.S.A.
Penguin Books Ltd, 27 Wrights Lane, London W8 5TZ, England
Penguin Books Australia Ltd, Ringwood, Victoria, Australia
Penguin Books Canada Ltd, 10 Alcorn Avenue,
Toronto, Ontario, Canada M4V 3B2
Penguin Books (N.Z.) Ltd, 182–190 Wairau Road,
Auckland 10, New Zealand

Penguin Books Ltd, Registered Offices:
Harmondsworth, Middlesex, England

First published by Signet, an imprint of New American Library,
a division of Penguin Books USA Inc.

First Printing, April, 1992
10 9 8 7 6 5 4 3

A
Cat by Any
Other Name

1

There were three Siamese kittens. Winken was on my head. Blinken was playing with my right thumb. And the third, Nod, was on the carpet in front of me, staring up at me with her profoundly sad eyes.

A second later they had all changed places, and I couldn't tell who was who.

The night was warm. The glass doors of the terrace were open and I could see out—over the East River and the lights of the Queensboro Bridge. Ava Fabrikant's Sutton Place apartment was magnificent; it nestled like a jewel in the ivy-covered building, twenty-three stories above the river.

We had eaten the orange duck, and now we were all waiting for the great moment. There was Ava, and her husband, Les. Barbara Roman, and her husband, Tim. Sylvia Graff, and her gentle alcoholic husband, Pauly. Renee Lupo and myself.

What was the great moment?

The serving of the peppermint tea.

Oh, not just any tea! Tea brewed from the first crop to come up in our community herb garden on the Lower East Side of Manhattan. Fifteen tiny peppermint leaves.

Three months before, one of my cat-sitting clients had told me about four women, all cat lovers, who were going to create a herb garden on a tiny parcel of wretched, garbage-strewn land, just off Avenue B.

They were, she told me, going to plant basil and coriander and dill and thyme and chamomile and peppermint. And, above all, they were going to plant catnip and calamint.

And then, along with schoolchildren from the area, they were going to harvest and dry the herbs, package them, and then sell them to gourmet food stores—with all the proceeds going to the ASPCA.

It struck me as the most romantic and quixotic of adventures. A herb garden in the city?

But why not? I hadn't dug into the earth since I left my grandmother's dairy farm to go to the big city almost twenty-five years ago. And I needed a change in my life. I needed something different . . . nontheatrical . . . basic.

So I called them and they welcomed me, and the last three months of planning and planting and fertilizing a small, desolate patch of urban earth had been glorious.

Barbara Roman sat down on the sofa beside me. Winken, Blinken, and Nod immediately switched their allegiance and overran her. Her laughter came out in peals.

She picked Blinken up with one hand and held the kitten close to her face.

"I wonder," she said, "what Swampy would make of you."

Swampy was her grizzled old tomcat. Then she kissed Blinken on the nose. That was too much, and off the kitten flew, the others following. Five seconds later they were lost to sight.

The sounds of gentle bickering over the brewing process wafted into the living room from Ava's immense kitchen.

"Hell hath no fury like middle-aged herb gardeners," Barbara nodded.

I laughed. I was beginning to pick up a faint odor of peppermint. I turned to Barbara to tell her, but she had already picked it up and was nodding happily. We were very much in sync.

Barbara was the first good friend I had made in twenty years. We spent hours on the phone together. She was interested in me: in my acting, in my cat-sitting, in my crime-solving, in the men who had shared my life. Barbara was literate and witty and good—but above all she had the gift of compassion. And I was not the only person who thought so. Everyone who knew this small brown-haired woman with a penchant for smocks loved her. And if they didn't, they listened to her because she made sense. Maybe she was, in the old-fashioned sense, wise.

She leaned over toward me. "Look at poor Renee." I looked across the room where Sylvia Graff's husband, Pauly, was telling Renee some kind of disjointed story.

"She's making believe she's listening, but her mind is on the peppermint tea," Barbara speculated.

A shout of triumph came from the kitchen and Ava appeared holding a tray. On the tray were eight beautiful little Japanese cups.

"Drum roll, please!" Ava shouted at her husband, Les, who did his best by rattling a fork against a piece of furniture.

Walking gingerly, as if she were carrying a priceless treasure, Ava approached the French Provincial dining table and carefully put the tray down.

We all rushed to the table. Each of us picked up a cup and held it high.

"Wait!" Les called out. "What about sugar?" He was greeted with looks of such withering scorn that he seemed to scrunch down into the carpet.

"A toast is definitely in order," Sylvia said.

"To the plant who sacrificed her fabulous leaves," Renee offered.

We drank. There were only two fingers' worth of tea in each cup.

After the great moment was over we placed the cups back onto the tray. No one knew what to say.

"Well," Ava finally said, "mine tasted like peppermint tea."

We all burst out laughing. There is nothing so ludicrous as searching for a superlative when it just isn't appropriate.

After the tea we had a delicious lemon mousse and strong French roast coffee and brandy.

The hours flew by. No one made any move to leave. At around eleven-thirty I found myself listening to Renee. Barbara stood next to me, sipping brandy. Behind her was Ava, coffee cup in hand.

"I read this fascinating article about trap-gardening," Renee said.

"What is 'trap'-gardening?" Ava asked, adding, "It sounds almost cruel."

Barbara handed me her brandy glass to hold. "I'll be right back," she said. "I want to get some air."

"Well," Renee continued, "imagine that you are growing potatoes. But each year that you've tried to grow them in the past, they've been decimated by potato beetles. What do you do if you're an organic gardener and refuse to use pesticides?"

"Pray?" asked Ava.

"No. You grow eggplant."

"And forget the potatoes?" I asked, confused.

"No. In addition to the potatoes. You see, there is only one crop potato beetles like better than potatoes—and that is eggplant. So, the beetles will decimate the eggplant and leave the potatoes alone." Renee's dark eyes flashed. She was a writer, and very intense. She seemed to see cosmic significance in the most mundane things.

"What is that noise?" Ava asked. There *was* a noise now—a growing sound of horns from the street below.

Les called out from the far side of the room. "There must be a backup on the East River Drive. Take a look out, Ava."

Ava handed me her coffee cup. I now had Barbara's brandy glass in one hand and Ava's coffee cup in the other. Ava walked out onto the terrace. I looked for a place to put the things down.

A horrible scream shattered the air around us.

It seemed to suck the air from the room.

It came from the terrace.

We ran out and saw Ava standing by the terrace ledge. Her hands were cupping her face. The scream lingered on, gurgling in her throat.

I stared down, out over the railing. The cars were backed up as far as the eye could see in either direction. Their headlights glowed like newly lit candles.

On the highway, far below, lay a small black object. It was a body.

We all looked around, furtively at first, then with increasing desperation.

Barbara Roman was not among us.

I looked at my trembling hand. The brandy glass

was still there. I walked slowly to the terrace wall and leaned against the brick.

Barbara had handed me her drink, walked out to the terrace, and leaped to her death.

2

Three days later was the funeral, if one could call it that. Barbara had left no written instructions, but she had told Tim once—long ago, he said—that she wanted to be cremated, so Tim arranged for cremation. He decided he would strew the ashes about the herb garden.

As agreed, we gathered in the garden at ten in the morning, all still in a state of shock. There were people there I didn't recognize. Barbara's friends? Relatives? I wasn't curious. What did it matter?

The morning was cloudy and warm. The plants seemed to be bending low in sympathy. Several neighborhood people stood just outside the make-shift fence and looked in—confused, a bit apprehensive, not knowing what was going on. I could see some of the children who had helped us with the planting, and a few of the homeless who had drifted in from Tompkins Square Park.

No one spoke. We stood and looked at one another, then at the pattern of the garden, then up at the adjoining tenements, smudges against the troubled sky.

Tim had arrived early, and now he stood on the far side of the garden perimeter, near the cat-nip. He wore a gray suit, gray shirt, and a black tie. In the crook of his arm was an odd-looking box. Next to Tim stood Ava Fabrikant, who kept touching his arm in a pathetic gesture and then taking her hand away. The rest of us fanned out along the edges of the garden.

To one side of me Renee Lupo stood. Obviously out of agitation, she constantly shifted her weight from one foot to the other. On my left was a young man I didn't know. He stared resolutely at a point on a brick wall nearby. He had haunted blue eyes and a few days' growth of beard.

For some reason—I suppose just to keep from losing control—I began to talk to the young man about the history of the building that had once stood on the lot where we were now assembled. I spoke quite softly, informing him that it had started out as a synagogue, then become a church, then housed a dance company, then been taken over by a drug rehabilitation clinic, then a theater troupe. Just before it was razed because of a fire, it had been a very loud and seedy bar. I even told him about the time, in the building's theater phase, when I had auditioned for a part in a play called *Where Is Emma Now?* I didn't even know whether the man was listening to me. He kept his eyes on the house across the way and just nodded from time to time. Then I stopped the monologue as abruptly as I had begun it. Renee Lupo had grabbed my hand. We both began to weep.

The first wave of true grief over the death of my friend hit me at exactly that moment. I realized, quite simply, that I would never again see her or hear her voice over the telephone for as long as I lived, and that realization, three days after the event, slammed into my body like a battering ram. I was afraid—so afraid I would fall that I reached out with my free hand and grasped the young stranger next to me by the arm, so that I was holding on to both him and Renee.

Suddenly I was ashamed. Embarrassment had replaced fear. I felt like a tall Raggedy Ann who was coming unstuffed. Sylvia Graff's husband Pauly and Ava's husband Les rushed over to me, each of them taking me by an arm and leading me away. We walked and walked, going nowhere. They said not a word. I tried to speak but found it hard—my breath was coming in short, cutting little bursts.

My numbing panic subsided in time. Tentatively, Pauly and Les released their hold on me. I smiled to let them know I was going to be all right, and on my own I started back to take my place in the circle of mourners.

Standing there, momentarily recovered from my sudden bouts of grief and panic and waiting for the ceremony to commence, I thought again for some reason of the play I had mentioned to the young man only a few moments before, *Where Is Emma Now?*

It had been one of those voguish philosophical murder plays. The character Emma never appeared onstage, because she was serving a life term in prison for murdering her three-year-old daughter.

The play itself consisted of dramatic interviews and monologues with those who loved and hated Emma, orchestrated by a Pirandello-type narrator who addressed the audience directly when he wasn't interrogating the characters.

I had auditioned for the part of Anya, Emma's psychiatrist. It was a good part, and I was disappointed when I didn't get it.

But my thoughts that morning, as I stood in that

sad herb garden, did not revolve around my failure
to land the part of Anya. I was remembering, instead, the part of the narrator who, after each interview with one of Emma's friends or lovers or
physicians, noted to the audience in flamboyant
style that life always imitates theater, but theater
has nothing to do with life.

It was all really just fluff then, just heady nonsense. But now, in the presence of my friend's
ashes and mourners, it didn't seem nonsense at
all.

I understood for the first time what the narrator
in the play had been saying: that the theater re-
veals the logic of human events. As *Where Is
Emma Now?* proceeds, we discover that Emma
probably did not kill her daughter. And then, after
the audience has been rocked by that bombshell,
we learn that Emma may not have even had a
daughter at all.

The logic of the theater is to strip away all the
given truths—to show that facts are baubles.

I looked around the garden at the faces of the
mourners.

My hands grew cold. It dawned on me that for
the first time since the tragedy, I had gone beyond
grief and entered a different reality.

I simply could not believe that what had happened had really happened. Oh, I believed that
Barbara had fallen to her death. And I knew that
even supposedly happy people kill themselves.
And I knew that evil things happen to good people.

No, it was the logic of the script that was peculiar—from the herb garden planting to the tea
party to the funeral. Something was very wrong.

Suddenly I felt ashamed at myself for all those

strange speculations. Logic? Theater? Shame on me. I was there to bid good-bye to my dearest friend. And besides, *Where Is Emma Now?* had closed after eleven performances.

I shut my eyes, and prayed to my own God that whatever part of Barbara still lived would be at peace.

Tim Roman stepped forward just then. He said in a booming voice: "I am glad you could all come today. Barbara would have wanted—" But suddenly his resolve crumbled and he began to weep horribly. We didn't know what to do, so we just stood there and watched him act out his pain.

It didn't last long. Tim held up his hand, and that seemed to help him regain control. Composed, he started his speech again, this time more quietly.

"This is where she would have wanted her ashes . . . um . . . planted." He stopped, laughing somewhat crazily. "I don't know . . . what does one do with ashes? Place them? Plant them? Dump . . . *Strew* them, I suppose." For a minute he stared, lost, at the box in his hands. Tim sighed deeply. "Oh, Barbara loved—but I guess I don't have to tell you how much she loved this garden. It was always on her mind. And you were always in her thoughts. She loved all of you so much."

Without further words, he opened the box and turned it over quickly. The powdery white substance fluttered out. There was so little of it. But we could see the ashes float on the air and disperse, almost as if someone had flicked a giant cigarette.

Tim snapped shut the lid on the box. All was quiet now. Even the persistent sounds of the city seemed to recede, like the last strains of the music at the end of a movie.

Some of the guests began to leave, making their way over to Tim to offer their condolences. I heard one woman whisper to a companion that she was surprised there had been no religious ceremony, that there should have been a minister—or *someone*—to say a few words. Or at least Tim should have said a prayer.

Renee suddenly wheeled in her place, away from the garden, and stared out at the street.

"So stupid . . . so inexplicable!" she said to me bitterly.

I watched her profile, her thin, dark face like a glove pulled tight.

"Do you understand what I am saying, Alice? She had everything to live for. *Everything*, period. She was loved. And she loved. Stupid! Stupid! Stupid! No meaning. No sense at all. One moment she's here with us, listening, laughing, talking. And then she's gone. There's no reason, Alice. Where's the reason? Oh, God, sometimes I hate this world!"

I couldn't dispute what Renee had said. And I didn't know how to comfort her. So I said nothing.

Renee turned back toward the garden. "Ashes!" she snorted. "How appropriate: ashes, *nothing*, specks landing on some effete little plants in the most godforsaken part of the city." She buried her face in her hands.

All I knew was that it was imperative I should be alone. I wanted to go back to my apartment and see my cats. That's all. I told Renee that I had to leave. Through the tears she nodded in assent. I walked briskly out of the garden and headed for

Second Avenue, quickening my pace as if to match the speed of the flashbacks reeling through my head.

In my mind I was back in Ava's apartment, and Barbara had handed me her brandy glass because she was going to get some air, she said.

"Alice!"

At first I thought the sound of my name was just part of the reverie.

"Alice! Wait!"

But no, it wasn't. When I stopped and turned I saw a figure running up the block toward me. It was Tim Roman.

He was approaching with frightening speed and purpose—at least it seemed that way. Running with abandon, desperation, as if catching up with me were the most important thing in his life, as if I had something of his that he had to retrieve at all costs.

He stopped five feet away from me, trying to catch his breath. The box was still in his hand.

Still breathing sharply, he asked: "Why are you leaving?"

"I need to rest for a while, Tim."

"Did you at least see the ceremony?"

I didn't know what he meant. Hadn't I just overheard a complaint about the distinct lack of ceremony? Then I realized he must be referring to the scattering of the ashes.

"Yes, I was there, Tim. Didn't you see me? I was standing next to Renee."

He regarded me strangely, as if he were puzzling out the meaning of the very simple words I'd just spoken.

Tim said something I couldn't hear. I moved closer. "What did you say, Tim?"

"I said, 'I don't . . . know . . . what . . . to do.' " He had spoken very slowly and carefully, and never in my life had I heard any sadder words.

"Tim," I began, then left it. "Poor Tim."

I kissed him gently on the cheek, backed up a few steps, turned, and started across the avenue.

"Just a minute!" he cried out. "Alice, I have something to give you!"

"What do you have to give me?"

"I have something to give you," he repeated, not answering my question.

I paused a minute before saying, "I have to go now, Tim. Call me—okay?"

The traffic light was with me at that moment. I took the opportunity to cross. When I reached the other side I looked back. He was still standing there, holding that box.

3

Tim didn't call me. Instead he simply appeared on my doorstep one afternoon. He was carrying *two* boxes this time.

His appearance put the seal on what had already been a difficult morning. I had spent the day up to that point trying to sell packets of dried catnip to gourmet shops and the fancier grocery markets in my neighborhood. We were all still reeling from Barbara's death, but we'd decided to carry on the work of the herb garden anyway, because Barbara would have wanted it that way. We maintained the division of labor that had been decided upon: We all harvested, but Sylvia and Ava dried the plants, and Renee packaged them, and me, I sold them. It was a task for which I would never have volunteered. But my sister gardeners had somehow come to the I suppose rather logical conclusion that an actress should make an ideal saleswoman.

By ten-thirty that morning I had already been in and out of four stores, without a sale.

My fifth stop was a brand-new, upscale health food store on Second Avenue. It was called Nature & Nurture. I walked in boldly, remembering Ava Fabrikant's pep talk, designed to assure me I'd be a successful salesperson. "But, Alice, you're an actress—remember? An *actress*. You know how to

make an entrance, right? You know how to per-
suade, inspire trust, charm. You'll just sweep in
grandly and turn it on. You'll blow the competition out of the water.''

"What competition is that?'' I asked.

"You'll be irresistible,'' she assured me.

But my grand entrance into Nature & Nurture
was wasted. The place was entirely devoid of people. It did look like a well-stocked operation however: jars and jars of organic, pesticide-free jams
and spreads . . . cans of scrupulously prepared
vegetarian soup . . . bottles of gargantuan mega-
vitamin tablets . . . racks of books on the subjects
of health and exercise and holistic healing . . .
even a small refrigerator stocked with bottles of
goat's milk and containers of mysterious murky
liquids whose labels were printed in colorful Japanese lettering.

I walked over to the deserted counter. How
quaint—there was a little bell. I gently tapped on
it, but the tinkle wasn't loud enough to rouse a
mouse. So I slapped it hard. I'll flip back into the
charm mode as soon as the proprietor appears, I
told myself.

"Coming, coming,'' I heard someone grumble
from the back of the store. A man appeared a minute after that. He was dressed in black T-shirt and
jeans, and was covered with dust. I noticed he was
carrying a pair of pliers and a light bulb, obviously
having been repairing something in back. He
didn't seem excited at the prospect of what, for all
he knew, was a paying customer.

"What can I do for you, miss?'' He ran his hand
through the wisps of graying red hair above his
round face.

By way of an answer, I took out one of the small packets from my shoulder bag and held it up. "I'd like to interest you in carrying our wonderful organic catnip. It's homegrown, right here in the city in a lovely herb garden downtown. It costs you only seventy-five cents a unit, and you could sell it easily for a dollar and a half or even two dollars a bag."

I guessed my pitch wasn't working, because he didn't reply. He looked from my face to the bag of catnip and then back at me. Before I could go on with my spiel, though, he began to laugh. Not just a chuckle but a huge laugh—one I might have appreciated if this had been a production of *Private Lives*, for instance.

I didn't understand. What had I done?

After a minute he composed himself. "I'm sorry. Please excuse me. It's just that I come out here like Jeeves the Butler, in answer to that ridiculous bell, and I see this tall, gorgeous woman in a forties suit jacket my mother would have killed for, and then you launch into a spiel about catnip, and then I realize you were Kate in the last play I ever took my mother to. It was all just too funny."

"You saw me in *Taming of the Shrew?*"

"The Cherry Lane. Nineteen seventy-one. You were exquisite."

"Well, aren't you nice? And you like my clothes, too."

He laughed again. "Guess you never know how things are going to turn out, right? I'm managing a rabbit-food emporium and you're pushing— I mean . . ."

"Yes," I jumped in. "Well, anyway, this really

is a fine product. Would you consider trying a few packages?''

''Look. Thanks, anyway. But we can't use it. There's a pet store around the corner. Why don't you try them?''

''I could leave it here on consignment,'' I pressed on, though I wanted nothing more than to be out of there. ''You pay nothing unless you sell it.''

''I'm sure we won't have any call for it.'' He shook his head. He was starting to walk away. I was losing him.

''One minute more!'' I called out, knowing now the literal meaning of ''Don't take 'no' for an answer.'' ''You do know, of course, that catnip is not just for cats?''

''What do you mean?''

''Did you know, for instance, that catnip was brought to the New World back in 1620 by a Captain Mason, who had selected it as one of the essential herbs to be planted in the gardens of Newfoundland fishermen?''

I'd done it now. But since he'd obviously already decided I was a nut, I went on. ''Why, the Romans used it for ailments of the nose and throat. The American colonists used it as a remedy for mild stomach disorders in children. And trappers used it to relieve poison ivy burns.''

I didn't know whether he believed all of it, but I knew then that I had him. I threw out, as a final flamboyant tidbit: ''In medieval Europe it was a common culinary herb for soups and stews. And surely you know how delicious and healthful it is as a tea?''

The man sighed, all the fight gone out of him. ''Leave a couple,'' he said, and he smiled again.

I stacked twenty packets neatly on the counter and left.

I began the walk home, exhausted.

As soon as I turned the corner onto Twenty-sixth Street I spotted Tim Roman on the stoop of my apartment building.

When he noticed me approaching he straightened, holding my eyes with his own until we were standing face-to-face. His face looked thinner, and his eyes were bloodshot. His wavy gray hair was a little mussed. For the first time, he looked his age—about fifty. But if there was about him a worn-down air, there was also one of sportiness—Tim looked almost rakish. His black turtleneck and overalls gave him a look of downtown artiness. Well, after all, he was a designer.

"I have something to give you," he said in a clipped voice, nodding at an oblong box lying on the step. But my eye went of its own accord to the other box: a cat carrier.

"That's not . . . Swampy?" I asked, incredulous. Was he going to give me Barbara's cat?!

"Yes, it is Swampy," he replied. "I thought you might spend a few minutes with him. He's become so morose since Barbara—I think he misses a woman's touch."

"But I have two cats upstairs, Tim. It wouldn't be fair—not to mention safe—to bring another cat into the house."

"Couldn't you put them in another room, just for a few minutes? I promise I won't stay long."

He was obviously still in the throes of grief. There was so much pain in his face that at that moment I would have done just about anything to rid him of it.

We climbed the stairs together, landing after landing, five flights in all. He waited outside while I herded my beasts into the small bedroom. Bushy was no problem; he was sleeping on the living room rug as usual, so I just plucked up the big Maine Coon in my arms and carried him down the hall and dropped him on the bed. He yawned and sought out the pillow. Pancho was another story. My no-tailed, scarred, gray ASPCA survivor was on one of his crazy runs through the apartment, in flight from imaginary enemies. I stationed myself at the door of the bedroom, and when Pancho flew by and into the room I shut the door behind him. Then I admitted Tim and his parcels.

Tim went to the sofa and sat down, wearily stretching out his long legs. His tiredness showed in his every movement. Grief takes a lot out of you—I knew. He closed his eyes and kept them that way for a long moment. I sat quietly in my chair.

Then he roused himself and bent down to open the door of the cat carrier.

Swampy ambled out. I had seen the cat before at Barbara and Tim's apartment, but I never ceased to marvel at him. Swampy was positively thuggish, the quintessential alley cat: a massive, low-framed beast with bright, confrontational eyes, a swaggering gait, and a short coat the blue-black color of a mean-looking gun.

"Barbara talked to him all the time," Tim said, "and now he has no one to communicate with." A case of classic projection, I thought smugly, although I never would have said so. Instead I began to speak to Swampy, holding my hand near his head so that he could sniff me. He seemed to be uninterested in what I had to say. He just continued to check out his new surroundings, maybe looking for trouble. Then I got an idea. I fetched one of the packets of catnip and hit him gently on the nose with it, allowing him to get a good whiff. That perked him up. I threw the packet behind the pillow on the sofa. Swampy leaped up and began to search.

With the cat happily engaged, Tim picked up his second package from the floor.

"Here, Alice," he said, extending it to me, handling the box as though it were a sacred object.

I placed the box on my lap and took off the lid. Inside were a pair of running shoes and a jogging outfit. I continued to look down at the items, not understanding their significance.

Tim leaned forward, pressing his strong, tapered fingers together. "They were Barbara's," he said quietly. "Alice, you know how much she thought of you. Barbara loved you. She'd want you to have something personal of hers, I just know she would."

I searched my mind for something to say. "I didn't know that Barbara was . . . I didn't know that she ran."

"Oh yes, for some time now. She ran every morning. Left the house at six and came back around eight. Then we'd have coffee together before I went to work." He looked off then, and I could see that he was crying.

"I think I'd better be leaving now," he said. Tim retrieved the cat and stuffed him into the box. "Thank you, Alice."

I sat looking at the clothing, shaking my head. Then I closed the lid of the box and stashed it in the hall closet. Weird. The events of the long day were starting to close in on me. I was tired, too. I heard the sounds of a disagreement in the bedroom, so I went in and released my two cats. I lay down with the radio on and fell into a somber, dreamless sleep.

4

"Earth to Swede. Earth to Swede. Come in, Alice! Where *are* you, girl?" Tony Basillio was waving his hand in front of my face.

We were sitting in a dark bar on Seventh Avenue in the twenties. It was a few minutes past noon.

"I'm sorry, Tony," I said, sipping from my club soda. "I'm distracted, I guess. Was I being rude?"

"I wouldn't say 'rude,' " he laughed, "but I just told you the best news I've had since I left my wife. Since I decided to chuck the copy stores. Maybe my only good news since you stopped—ahem—sleeping with me. And you just sit there like you've lost your best friend."

He had just finished an exuberant story about the big break he'd received. He'd landed the job as stage designer for a far-out, modern-dress production of *Julius Caesar,* at the American Shakespeare Festival in Stratford, Connecticut. The original group was long extinct, but a new company had been formed and were using the old theater. Excited at being back in the theater milieu, he couldn't wait to get to work. He was leaving the City for Connecticut in a couple of days.

I had to smile ruefully at the inadvertent sick joke he'd just made. "Truth is, Tony, I *did* lose my best friend. Just about my best friend."

"What do you mean?"

I gave him the capsule version of recent events. He had known, of course, about my work at the herb garden, thought all of it was hilarious, but I had not spoken much about my friendship with Barbara and what she had come to mean to me. I don't really know why I'd never told him how close we'd become—perhaps because I thought he'd be jealous. I depended heavily on Tony's friendship, too.

He paled. "Oh, God. I really put my foot in it, didn't I?" he said. "Swede, I'm so sorry." And he leaned over and kissed me.

It was only when he leaned back that I noticed he was letting his hair grow long again. His thin face, handsome but pockmarked, and his deep-set eyes made him look rather like an aging addict. He would be pleased, I thought, to know that he was beginning to look like Julian Beck, or better, Artaud.

I wanted to bring the conversation back to him. "So who's directing?" I asked. "Some young turk?"

But he didn't answer. "How did your friend . . . ?"

"She went off an apartment terrace. Twenty-three stories up. Or was it twenty-five? I forget."

He took in a sharp breath and covered his eyes. "Jesus, Swede. Did you see her . . . afterwards?"

"No, no. I didn't." The smell of frying meat drifted across the little booth. I swallowed a couple of times before going on. "The problem is, Tony . . . it just shouldn't have been Barbara. Anyone else, but not her. Do you know what I mean?"

"No, I'm not sure I do."

"I mean, not *her*. I just can't stand that it was

her." My voice broke suddenly, and he sat there, letting me cry as long as I needed to.

Tony had long ago finished his second vodka and Coke. It was time for him to leave. He wrote a telephone number on a slip of note paper and handed it to me. "That's where I'll be in Connecticut. I'm there for you. If you need me, just call."

We walked outside and stood together in the warm afternoon sun.

"Life is sweet," he said, "but it sucks. Right, sweetheart?"

I had to laugh at that.

He squeezed my hand, turned and headed uptown. I watched him go, then began to walk east.

The moment I was inside the apartment door I kicked off my shoes. Bushy walked by me casually—a sure sign I'd interrupted some mischief. I greeted him warmly just the same.

Ah, Tony. He had turned out—as mercurial as he was—to be a sort of rock for me, a real anchor in life. When he was as understanding and lovely to me as he had been today, I tended to lose sight of why I'd broken off the sexual end of our relationship. As I took off the rest of my things I thought of all the men with whom I'd once been in love, or what passes for it, and how sooner or later they'd all become just amiable luncheon or cocktail companions. What does that say about me? I wondered. "Oh, well," I leaned down and confided to the cat, "you know they're in love if they take you to dinner." It sounded like the hit song from a very bad musical.

Perhaps when all is said and done I really am a cockeyed optimist, speaking of musicals. It was as though I were determined to extract something light and good out of what was decidedly a downbeat day. I felt the aching need for a few laughs and some honest girl-talk with a friend, so, standing in my stockinged feet, I picked up the phone and started to dial—incredibly, insanely—Barbara Roman's number. I slammed down the receiver before reaching the last digit.

Oh, Lord. The sense of loss was as fresh as ever, the stunning, uncomprehending grief, the just plain missing her.

It was at that moment, sitting on the sofa with my head in my hands, that I thought of Tim Roman's ridiculously bizarre gift to me. I hurried to the closet and retrieved the cardboard box. As I sat examining the things inside it Bushy leaped up for a cursory inspection, then just as quickly decided he wasn't interested. Barbara might well have appreciated the absurdity of the memento of her that Tim had passed on to me—the wild inappropriateness of it—or she might simply have been appalled at his lack of taste and sensitivity.

I unfolded the jogging outfit. It was a satiny one-piece affair that zipped up the front, neither old nor new. It had been laundered a few times, clearly, but had none of the well-worn softness of the gardening overalls and smocks that Barbara wore so frequently. There were no pulled threads, no fraying at the cuffs, no discoloration from sweat. I ran my hand over the fabric again and again, almost as if I might bring forth some spark of energy.

Then I took one of the shoes out of the box. The label on the back read ADDIDAS. A blue lady's sneaker with sky-blue laces. I turned it over in my hand. That was odd: The tread on the bottom of the shoe was not worn down at all. Again, not a new item, but obviously not a much-used one, either.

I pulled out the other shoe, delaying for just a few seconds my inspection of its heel and sole, making a little routine of the suspense. Same deal.

I sat there thinking, the things still in my lap. How do you go out running every morning for months and not wear down your shoes? How do you manage to keep the clothes you jog in looking almost pristine? You don't. It would be understandable if the suit and shoes were new and there simply hadn't been time enough to break them in thoroughly. But these items weren't new. . . . Well, they were and they weren't.

I got up and went over to the window, the pace of my thoughts as quick and ragged as the steps of the people on the five o'clock street below.

By the time I found myself standing at the sink, washing spinach leaves for supper, the sundry speculations I'd been turning over in my head had cohered into absolute certainties. As far as I was concerned there were no more could-be's or maybe's—I had settled on the cold, hard facts.

Those "facts" were these: Barbara Roman left the house at about six each morning dressed for an invigorating run, and she returned home a few hours later. And every day that she put those clothes on and walked out the door, she was lying to her husband.

Why would she have told Tim that she was out jogging, when she was not? Answer: Barbara had had something to hide. The obvious was obvious. Facts were facts.

So Barbara had had a lover. Why did that so

astonish and shock me? I didn't think of myself as
a prude, but perhaps the farm girl in me
was coming to the surface here, where Barbara
was concerned. Loads of married women have affairs—not to mention married men. Why was the
thought of Barbara doing what millions of others
had done so unacceptable? Had I not only admired
and loved her but enshrined her? Granted her
sainthood? Yes, of course I had. The fact of the
matter was that I had put her up on all kinds of
absurd pedestals. Maybe we all had idealized her,
paying so much homage to her specialness that we
wouldn't allow her to be normal. Except that she
was special; she *was* different; we hadn't been
wrong.

A seamy image came to me then: Barbara in the
arms of some well-built young man in a dumpy
hotel. Or maybe it wasn't like that. Maybe he was
a debonair millionaire with an East Side townhouse. Sure . . . Barbara trotting delicately down
the street in her little pink outfit and shoes, turning the corner onto Second Avenue, jumping into
a waiting taxi, and speeding to his place each
morning. Him watching for the car from a high
window, and then the two of them spending the
early-morning hours making love in his spare
white bedroom.

This sort of thing may have been the stuff of
dreams for some middle-aged women, but I was
neither titillated nor amused by it. I was, however,
angry. I recognized suddenly that I was angry as
hell at Barbara. I couldn't think of a single thing
about my life that I wouldn't gladly have told her.
But she, on the other hand, had kept this enormous secret from me. Enormous and vital secret,
obviously. She'd jumped to her death because of

him, hadn't she? He—whoever he was—had left her, and so she'd killed herself. No. Impossible. I was in Soap Opera Land. Nobody in this day and age commits suicide over something like that.

Perhaps the lover was dead, then? And she'd acted out of grief for him?

Or perhaps the fact of her lover was the least of her secrets. He was only the tip of an iceberg. Barbara had another life altogether—one hidden from family and friends—and the lover was only one part of it. And something in that second life had driven her to destroy herself. Was the soap opera taking over again? Was any of this possible?

One thing I *wasn't* making up: Barbara was dead. So, double life or no, who was going to benefit from my finding out why she jumped off that terrace? Why should I bother to find out why?

Because.

I had finished my instant coffee, and after washing up the dinner things I went after a brandy. Sitting there, feeling all alone in the dark city, I knew I was committed to getting answers to all the why's about Barbara's death. Even if I had to repress the distinctly uncomfortable feeling that I was invading her privacy, trampling on her rights, maybe even defiling the grave of a saint. I had to know, it was as simple as that, even if I never told another soul.

Because, I thought, as I checked to make sure that the front door was bolted. And as I felt a few tears stinging behind my eyelids, even I realized what a petulant, childish kind of non-answer that was.

I switched off the lamp. Making my way toward the bedroom in the dark, I heard the cats, who'd been roosting god knows where, fall into step behind me.

I had never been a soap opera fan. I was as grounded in reality as the next actress. And I knew with total certainty that I had not merely imagined that Barbara Roman loved and trusted me.

I drifted off to sleep knowing that I had my work cut out for me, and thinking also about Basillio's earlier flippancy. Life is sweet, but it sucks. And vice versa.

Because!

5

I rose very early, with the sky just beginning to lighten over the top of the high-rise across the way. The cats of course thought nothing of the earliness of the hour—as soon as my feet had hit the floor, they wanted to be fed.

There was still some of Pancho's favorite snack in the refrigerator—saffron rice—so I mixed it liberally with his regular food and watched him feast—even though I was on a tight schedule.

It was always a joy to watch Pancho in one of his rare moments of repose. As for the saffron rice, I admit that it's a very strange taste for a cat. Since I had obtained him from the ASPCA, which was located on the fringes of Spanish Harlem, I always thought of it as meaning that Pancho had spent his childhood with a Hispanic family. Hence the liking for saffron rice. But saffron is an Indian seasoning for the most part, so I never could be sure. A scientific inquiry would have demanded that I give him rice without saffron and then a saffron-flavored food other than rice, to see which element in saffron rice he craved. But I never experimented.

While Bushy ate leisurely, Pancho ate warily. He was tense. His long gray body, with the large ugly scar on the right flank from some ancient wound, was poised to escape if his nonexistent enemies came too close. His strange yellow eyes flicked back and forth. His rust-colored whiskers twitched ever so slightly.

"Good, isn't it, Pancho? You must admit I take care of you," I told him. Did I detect a slight movement of what was left of his tail in response? Maybe. Poor Pancho. The loss of his tail had probably happened when he was a small kitten. He had obviously led a very difficult and a very dangerous life.

"No one will ever hurt you here, Pancho," I assured him for the millionth time.

Time was fleeting. I had to dress. But something about Pancho that morning kept me glued there. Something odd.

I studied him as he ate. And then it dawned on me: He had grown gaunt again. Once again his ribs had begun to show. Just like when I had brought him home from the ASPCA.

"Your ribs are sticking out again, Pancho!" I exclaimed. I was just about to stroke him when I caught myself, realizing it would be cruel to interrupt his feast.

In the first three months of living with me, after I had rescued him from the gas chamber, Pancho ate voraciously. I mean he ate *anything* and *everything*—like a feral cat.

But as time passed, I realized that something was very wrong. No matter how much he ate, he didn't gain any weight. He stayed gaunt. His ribs continued to stick out. So when I took him to the vet for some shots, I mentioned it. They did some blood tests on Pancho. Lo and behold, Pancho was diagnosed as having a pancreatic insufficiency. His pancreas didn't produce a sufficient amount of digestive enzymes. So for the longest time I had to give him supplements, and finally the gauntness vanished.

"Pancho," I informed him sadly, "sooner or later you're going to have to visit the vet again. Sorry."

He didn't appear concerned. And I had other work to do.

By five-thirty I was out of the apartment and flagging down a cab. I took it up to the corner of Sixty-seventh Street and First Avenue.

Manhattan is most strange at that time of morning. All the hustle and energy has gone underground, all the threats are hidden. Everything is kind of clamped down.

I had pulled my long hair back into a basic spinster's bun. I was wearing sneakers, a pair of brown slacks, and a tan turtleneck. No jewelry, no scarves, no handbag. The lack of womanly hindrances gave me the desired aura of sleek, pared-down efficiency—a woman geared up for the task at hand.

But even with the tough lady-detective image put to one side, my purpose was indeed focused: to find out, somehow, where Barbara Roman had gone and what she had done after leaving her apartment building each morning around six dressed in a jogging outfit. For a moment, standing there alone on the deserted street corner, I felt not just peculiar but utterly silly . . . and not a little guilty. I knew that I was prying into things, in the wake of Barbara's death, that she, in life, had chosen to keep secret. But the mind of Alice Nestleton, girl detective, was made up. Okay, I couldn't bring my friend back to life, but I was going to discover the truth behind her suicide.

I patted the back pocket of my corduroy slacks.

The snapshot was there, a Polaroid one of the East Village neighbors had taken of the five of us in the first days of the herb garden. In the picture, four of us—Ava, Sylvia, Renee, and I—all held up garden implements so that they formed a kind of wreath over Barbara's head. She beamed out at the camera, looking like a happy, be-laureled child. Yes, I think that was Barbara's special grace: to seem both innocent and very wise, sophisticated yet guileless.

The Romans had lived in the hulking old red-brick building just off First Avenue. It had been their home for most of their marriage. I waited on the corner for a few more minutes, my eye on the red building.

At ten past six a dark-skinned man emerged from one of the side entrances, pulling an immense plastic trash bag behind him. He lugged it to the curb and left it there. He went back into the building and a few minutes later appeared with another bag, repeating the activity again and again until there were seven parcels lined up curbside for the sanitation men to pick up. He stopped to rest, lighting a cigarette.

I walked swiftly over to him. "Excuse me."

He looked up, startled, his eyes boring out of a sweat-stained face. The man was swarthy, and much shorter than I.

"Excuse me," I repeated. "I was wondering if you knew Barbara Roman? She was a tenant in your building."

"Yeah," he answered. "Yeah, I knew Mrs. Roman." He spoke with a slight Hispanic accent. "Some nice lady," he added. Then the inevitable cynical New York shadow crept across his face. "What do you want?"

"I was a good friend of hers," I said quickly, struggling for a coherent story. The man's obvious regard and affection for Barbara had thrown me. "We're putting together a little memorial service for her, and I wanted to talk to people in the neighborhood who knew her. You know, how she spent the day, where she shopped, all that sort of thing."

He wasn't following my confused cover story, and with good reason—it made little sense. So I went on talking: "She jogged every morning, didn't she?"

"Jogged?"

"Yes, running, you know."

"Oh, sure. I see her . . . saw her . . . every morning. About this time."

"And which direction did she run in?"

"Well, you couldn't really say she 'ran.' She would walk to Second Avenue and then go uptown. I figure she was heading for the park and would do her running there. I used to tell her, 'Be careful, be careful. You don't know what kind of crazy people in that park.' But every day, she went. Nothing ever happened, I guess."

He finished his cigarette and flicked the butt out onto the street.

"Lady," he said, not meeting my eyes, "let me ask *you* one thing."

"Yes?"

"You know Mrs. Roman well, right?"

I nodded.

"Did she really . . . jump? Off a building?" He asked it slyly, as if he were curious but also afraid, ashamed.

"Yes, she did," I said. "And thank you."

I walked to Second Avenue and turned north. Now what?

I decided to take the east side of the avenue first. Not many stores were open at this hour—a few luncheonettes, the dry cleaner, the newsstand, the all-night Korean green market.

I walked into each of the stores, showed the snapshot of Barbara, supposedly identifying her as a missing person, and asked if the proprietor knew her or could recall when he'd last seen her. I was trying to see the pattern of her neighborhood routine, trace her steps. I stopped in at every open establishment up to Seventy-second Street, then crossed over to work the west side of the avenue. This was a long shot, and really tedious work—especially since I'd have to come back at another time to interview everyone whose shop was not yet open—but it was the only way I could think of to proceed at six o'clock in the morning.

In a place called The Healthy Bagel—a little breakfast restaurant with a counter in the back and a few spindly tables near a front window that could have used a good washing—I found my first reward. Perhaps the long shot was going to pay off after all.

The Asian man behind the counter actually took the photograph out of my hands, saying, "I was wondering where she been."

"Then you've seen her here?"

"One egg over," was his answer. "Bagel toasted no butter schmeer scallion cream cheese on the side black coffee. Every day."

Every day. He knew her order by heart.

"Hope she turns up okay," he added. He had no reason to question my story that she was a "missing person."

I took the cup of coffee I'd ordered and went to one of the tables in the front. So, obviously, my scenario had to be at least half-right. No cab waiting to whisk her off to the rich guy's townhouse, but she hadn't been out jogging, either. No one about to take a two-hour run would breakfast on food like that. Maybe she would have a leisurely breakfast and then walk to the park, where he was waiting for her?

At any rate, I now had the first piece of her morning routine, the first six blocks of the route. She left the apartment, walked to Second, crossed over to the west side of the avenue and went north to Seventy-first Street, where she breakfasted at the questionably named Healthy Bagel. Then what?

It was going to take days, possibly weeks, to interview every store owner or employee in the neighborhood; I'd have to catch different people at different times of the day. And I couldn't stop there, of course. There were neighborhood acquaintances, bus drivers perhaps, maybe even the more civil homeless people who had little else to do but watch the world go by.

There was one other option for today's research: to stay put here in the restaurant for a while and see if any of the regulars knew Barbara, had talked to her, or noticed where she went when she left the Healthy Bagel.

They straggled in—the truck drivers, the cabbies, the young mothers who didn't work, all sorts of people. Those who ordered food and coffee to go I didn't bother with. To the few who sat down to eat I showed the photo and asked the rote questions. They couldn't recall her.

In a while an old woman, whom I'd seen harnessing her dog to a parking-meter pole outside, entered the restaurant and sat down at a table with her coffee and cake. She was somewhat over-dressed for the spring weather, her clothing that mixture of trash and treasure that single old ladies so often sport. Her hat, a kind of toque, probably one of those items from Tibet or Morocco that they hawk on the sidewalks downtown, was set off by a lovely rhinestone feather I certainly wouldn't have minded owning. She ate her cake with a fork, nibbling it as she gazed solicitously out at her old brown dog.

I slid off my seat and approached her. "Ma'am, I wonder if I could ask you to look at this photograph and tell me if you recognize this woman. She ate here every morning." I placed the Polaroid next to her plate, my thumb near Barbara's face.

"Barbara!" she exclaimed. "Where is she?"

"She's missing," I said. "We're trying to locate her."

The old lady sighed enormously. "I've been waiting and waiting for her. We ate together every morning. Maybe she's in the garden—have you looked there?"

I made certain I registered no surprise at her knowledge of the garden. "Yes, ma'am, we have."

"Well, if she isn't here and she isn't in the garden, she must be at church."

"Church?"

She glared suspiciously at me then, as if I must be a charlatan if I didn't know about this church.

"Well, of course," her voice grew a little harder. "She went there every morning when she left here."

I had to admit, I was no longer so completely in control of my reactions. "What church would that be?" I asked.

"Around the corner," she replied testily. Then she added, speaking slowly because there was an idiot across from her, "St. John's. The Roman Catholic . . . church . . . around . . . the corner."

It turned out that Edie—that was the old lady's name—knew quite a few things about Barbara's life, even if they weren't the kind of deeply intimate things I knew about her background. She knew that Barbara had a husband and a cat named Swampy. That Barbara had founded and worked in a downtown garden. That she was an animal lover and a sweet, kind person. And—unless Edie was putting me on, or crazy—she knew Barbara to be a regular churchgoer.

Barbara had never once spoken to me of God or religion—hers or anyone else's. She had mentioned in passing that Tim had been raised a Presbyterian, but neither of them had been to church in more than twenty years, except to hear the occasional Christmastime concert or oratorio. We had talked about everything under the sun, or so I thought—sex and death, career, love, theater, cats, plants, parents, decorating—but Faith, never.

I slid the photo back into my pocket. And I noticed that Edie was pointing her fork at the fly-specked wall clock over my head.

"Past seven o'clock," she said. "It's already started."

"What has?"

Edie seemed a little more kindly inclined toward me now. "Mass, dearie," she explained.

"Barbara always left in time for seven o'clock Mass."

I walked the block to Seventy-second Street and turned west. The church was just past the corner. The board outside said that weekday morning Mass was held at 7:30, 8:00, and 8:30. There was no 7:00 A.M. Mass. I was perplexed, to be sure, but somehow not surprised.

I walked up the great stone stairs and opened the heavy door. Same thought as earlier: Now what?

The church was dim and cool and damp. And so much bigger and more imposing than it looked from the outside. A few people were scattered throughout the pews. They were in various degrees of prayer and contemplation, oblivious to me. Candlelight shone on the statues of the mournful saints. The ceiling rose high above a resplendent altar, where a single priest in full vestments stood. He seemed to be arranging papers in a missal.

I walked quietly but purposefully down the aisle, feeling oddly oppressed by the high solemnity of it all, until I stood next to the priest.

"Father . . ." I began. That was right, wasn't it? You could address any priest as "Father."

"Father, I'm Alice Nestleton. May I ask you some questions?"

The priest looked at me. He was not a young man, but there was vitality in his cool green eyes and a solidity to his big body, even with a paunch showing through his robes. He smiled, nodding his pure white head.

"Well," he said gently, "my name is Father

Baer. And yes, you may ask me any question you like.''

It occurred to me then that he was probably expecting a query about St. Peter or fasting or proper behavior in the confessional. I hoped he wouldn't be too disappointed.

"Do you know this woman?" I brought the picture up close to his face, pointing to the grinning Barbara.

"Yes, I know Barbara Roman." He did not touch the photograph. "Has she been ill?"

"Why do you ask that?"

He looked at me for a long moment, no doubt evaluating my motives. Finally he said, uncomfortably, "Are you a friend or relative of Barbara's?"

"A very good friend," I answered.

"Is she in some sort of trouble?"

"A great deal," I said, not worried about the lie—not even a lie, really, more like a paradox. After all, death was about the biggest trouble a person could ever be in. But at the same time, the dead were beyond all trouble. "Please tell me, Father, how you know Barbara. Please."

"Something's happened." It wasn't a question. He stated it as fact. I nodded in affirmation.

"Barbara was taking instruction with me in the Catholic faith. She came in every morning at seven, before the seven-thirty Mass. She told me she wished not to tell her husband about it until after formal conversion, so she pretended to go out jogging in the mornings. I advised her to tell him now, but she wanted it the other way."

I was so astonished by his words that I sat down at the end of the aisle, saying nothing.

"Is there anything I can do for Barbara? I want her to—"

"She's dead."

Father Baer brought his hands together up near his mouth, the pain and amazement seeming to flow from his face right into his clenched fingers.

"What happened . . . to Barbara?" he finally said. "When?"

"About ten days ago. She killed herself."

"No. Oh, no," he spluttered, indignant. "That cannot be true."

"Do you think I would lie about such a thing!" I knew that I was fairly shouting at the priest.

But then I felt him touch me gently, just for a second, on my shoulder.

Calmer now, he said, "I just find that very difficult to believe. You see, Barbara was new to the Church, but very devout. She was serious about instructions, knew the Church's teaching on suicide. She was just short of conversion. She would not kill herself. She would *not.*"

I remained in the pew, ignoring the Mass that was still in progress. Only when the communicants started to move forward to receive the Eucharist from Father Baer did I rise from my seat, move past the others in my row, and head up the aisle toward the towering church door.

So, my imagination really had been mired in the mud of Soap Opera Land. There was no secret lover. Well, there was . . . but not one of this world. Barbara had been filled with the love of God, a love of life, and a newfound love of her Church-to-be. And if Father Baer was to be believed, all these precluded the possibility that she had taken her own life. His words still echoed in my ears: *She would not.*

I understood it dimly, only dimly. But I knew, as I'd known, somewhere inside me, all along, that the priest was right. She would not. She did not. I was there that night. I didn't see it happen, but Barbara was pushed off that terrace.

Someone had murdered my friend.

I walked back to Second Avenue and headed downtown. And there was Edie, struggling with the knot on her dog's leash. Briefly I toyed with the idea that I should stop and tell her that Barbara was dead. I knew that would be the right and decent thing to do, but I just couldn't bring myself to do it. I strode past her without stopping. But at the corner, I turned to look back at her in her Tibetan hat. Bent over that way, tugging at the patient animal's rope, she seemed so fragile. I started back. After all, Edie was old and alone. She needed help. And so did I.

6

I called Basillio. I'd found his Stratford number, dialed it, he'd answered, and there I sat with the receiver in my hand, talking. In other words, all the elements of a conversation were present—except that he wasn't listening to a single thing I said.

Instead, his responses smacked of the high-handed born-again. He was back in the milieu of the church-of-the-theater, and all else was nonsense. I wanted to talk about the murder I had uncovered, and he wanted to analyze me out of it.

"Swede, you're grief-stricken," he said, "and people in the throes of an overwhelming emotion like grief can become paranoid—at the very least, paranoid—and even delusional."

"What on earth," I asked acidly, "is that supposed to mean, Tony?"

"It means," he said languidly, "that your friend killed herself and you're unwilling to confront that fact."

I hated that tone! It was as if he were deigning to roll a few pearls of wisdom my way while he reached for an apple in a fruit basket, or a woman on a divan.

"Barbara committed suicide," he reiterated. "Don't you see that you're insisting that she *didn't* because the fact that she *did* is some kind of commentary . . . some kind of judgment . . . on your friendship with her? Your ego won't let you admit that you couldn't save her, that you failed her. But it isn't true, Swede. It wasn't your—''

That's when I hung up. Then I grabbed Bushy and held on to him for a while.

Of course I understood Tony's point: that it made me feel better to think Barbara had been murdered than to think she'd taken her own life. That way, no finger could be pointed at me. It was a fairly elementary analysis. That doesn't mean I accepted it, however. If there was any ego stuff going on, it was that I thought *I* could discover why Barbara had killed herself—when no one else could. And then I'd been brought up short by the very strong possibility that she hadn't killed herself at all.

I looked at my grandmother's old green jade clock, meant to sit on a mantelpiece, I suppose; it was ugly as sin, but rather valuable. It was two in the afternoon, give or take a few minutes. Unbelievable—just seven hours ago I was talking to Father Baer, receiving the stunning news about Barbara's religious conversion. I was still agitated. I'm no ingenue in regard to crime—it takes a great deal to discombobulate me. But the shock waves of this case—and it was strange to think of Barbara's death as a ''case''—were hitting me so hard they felt like an assault on my professionalism. And my ego? Damn that Basillio.

He was useless now as a sounding board, and that was exactly what I needed: someone to talk to, run my ideas by, help me piece things together. I needed a dialogue . . . a kind of Socratic encounter.

So, preposterously, Detective Rothwax of the NYPD came to mind. On the other hand, why *not*

him? We had worked together during my brief stint
as consultant for the Department's major-crimes
unit, RETRO. Granted, they had fired me. But in
the end it was I who solved their most perplexing
case: the Egyptian Cat Murders, in which the killer's practice had been to leave a toy mouse beside
each corpse.

I saw Detective Rothwax as a chance I should
take. He always left the Centre Street office around
four in the afternoon, unless he was working outside. But even when he was busy with legwork, he
usually came back in the afternoon for at least a
few minutes.

I left the apartment and splurged on a cab to
Centre Street. Then I stationed myself right next
to the revolving doors and waited. The streets
pulsed with the legal system's usual mix of titans
and mendicants: the wily cops, the up-and-coming
lawyers, the hollow-eyed accused.

About the time that the hot-dog vendor was closing up his cart for the day, Rothwax emerged,
alone, looking just a little weary around the edges.
He was wearing his customary outfit, a business
suit that was spiffy but very much out of fashion.
It was ten past four.

He walked past without noticing me. I caught
up with him at the curb.

"A minute of your time, Detective?" I said de-
murely.

He turned quickly, and his eyes widened in surprise. "I'll be damned! It's Cat Woman! How the
hell are you?" At least he didn't look unhappy to
see me.

"I'm well, Detective. Just fine."

"Everybody at RETRO keeps asking what happened to you. They don't know whether to look

for your name in the drama reviews or the police blotter.''

I obliged with the little chuckle he was looking for. It had been months since I'd seen him, or anyone else from RETRO. But he looked exactly the same, down to the scant number of wispy hairs to be found on his balding head.

''I need some help,'' I confided, and gestured to one of the empty stone benches that line the small park adjacent to the building. ''Why don't we sit?''

''You need help,'' he mused. ''And I thought the Cat Woman,'' he boomed in a mock-heroic voice, ''always worked alone.''

But he followed me to the bench and sat listening without any further teasing or jokes. I outlined the events leading to the ''suicide''—the peppermint tea party; the last few moments I had spent with Barbara; the scream; the realization that the speck on the road below was my friend; Tim Roman's delivery of the jogging paraphernalia—everything up to and including my talk with the priest and the conclusions I had drawn about Barbara's death.

Having heard me out, Rothwax was staring down at his nails.

''Alice, you've lost me.''

''Where?'' I asked, suspicious.

''You've lost me, Feline One.'' His eyes met mine then. ''Are you really saying that just because a woman was taking instructions in Catholicism, it must mean that she was murdered? Is that what you're saying?''

''No, Detective, I'm not. I'm just saying that my friend Barbara Roman, having embarked on instructions in a faith that says thou shalt not kill

yourself, would not kill herself. That's just the way
it is. And if she didn't jump off the terrace of her
own volition, then someone else pushed her.''

Tonelessly, he asked, ''What did the autopsy
say?''

''There wasn't one.''

''Um,'' he grunted. ''Well, it still may not prove
anything, but you could get a court order to dig
her up.''

''We can't 'dig her up.' She was cremated.''

A little smile crossed his lips then, and he turned
his hands palms-up. ''Game's over, CW. Fat lady
just sang.''

I managed not to reveal the irritation I was feeling and pressed on. ''What could the autopsy have
shown, if there had been one? Could it have proved
she was forced off the terrace?''

''Not at all. But it might have shown that she
was drunk or something. Or shown some other
trauma not connected to a fall . . . like a knife
wound.''

''Oh . . . Well, as I said, she was cremated.'' I
sat without speaking, looking pathetic.

''Let me just ask you this,'' Rothwax said with
a sigh. ''Is there a single other person who was at
the peppermint party who thinks she was murdered?''

''No,'' I hissed, ''of course not. Only me.''

Rothwax threw his head back. ''This sounds like
a case for . . . *CAT WO-MAN*,'' he bellowed and
meow-ed.

I could tell that he immediately regretted this
last bit of insensitivity, because he was suddenly
somber when I reached over and placed my hand
on his arm.

''I know you don't mean to be cruel,'' I said.

"And I know what I'm saying may not sound convincing to you. But I . . . loved . . . her very much. She was a great friend."

"Okay." He let my hand rest where it lay. "Okay. Then listen to me. Remember a while ago—that dumb conversation we had about the wisdom of the street? How you know how to do certain things real good, but I can do a lot of other things even better? Because I know the difference, intuitively, between the good guys and the bad guys? Remember?"

"Yes."

"Well, Alice, as a guy of flawless intuition, I'm here to tell you that you're way off base on this one. You don't have a prayer—no pun intended—of convincing anyone that your friend was murdered. You may have a little ego problem, but you're a very good investigator; and I may rib the hell out of you, but I know that you are. But right now, you're so hurt and sad about your friend that you're not thinking straight. You're confusing your feelings with the facts."

"But maybe we don't have all the facts. Why can't anyone see that?"

"You have enough of them, CW."

I tried interrupting again, but he talked on.

"Facts versus feelings! You've gotta sort them out. Like that nonsense with the priest. That's nothing, Alice. It's trivia. It's like a lot of bits and pieces of steel wool. Nothing . . . You get it?"

I pulled my hand back slowly. Rothwax was correct about one thing and one thing only—the bit about sorting things out. For instance, he was a cop, and I'd lost sight of that for a while. He was a cop and not a shrink, a cop and not an advisor, a cop and not Socrates. Socrates would have considered the possibility of just about anything before he shot you down.

I'd turned to two different men I trusted—Basillio and Detective Rothwax, who stood in radically different relations to me—and they'd both ended up telling me that I was grieving for a dead friend. Big news. Big insight. I knew bloody well what I felt, but that didn't make me feeble-minded—or wrong.

"I have to go," I said to Rothwax. "Thanks for your time. And give my best to everyone at RETRO."

But I didn't move off the bench.

"Everyone including Judy Mizener?"

"Sure," I said. I bore no ill feelings anymore toward the head of RETRO, who had dismissed me from the case. She had turned out to be a very smart, ambitious, and commendable woman . . . almost, one might add, a friend.

Rothwax stood up, inclined his head, and gave a courtly half bow. "See you around, CW."

It was all too clear that I was alone on this one.

A little bit of the anger I'd just felt over Rothwax's relentless teasing resurfaced. I had half a mind to show him—and Tony—what a well-placed paw with a sharpened claw can do to that anatomical spot where the male ego resides.

7

The morning sun was brilliant, robust, cleansing. And the ragged old tenements seemed to be gift-wrapped in its buttery light.

I was standing at the gate of the herb garden, looking on silently at the other women as they toiled. Renee hovered over the dill. Ava was in the far bed with the coriander. And Sylvia was weeding in our main cash crop—catnip.

I was going to have to be cautious and gentle with these three women, who had loved Barbara just as I had. But I would eventually have to tell them that it looked as though our friend had been murdered. Which wouldn't be nearly so difficult as telling them that they all made excellent suspects. One of them had probably killed her, unless . . . unless I was precisely the grief-stricken, paranoid egomaniac I'd been accused of being.

I entered the garden, closed the gate behind me, and walked over to Renee. She noticed me approaching and beckoned wildly to me.

"Quick, Alice! You've got to see this. Bend down here and look."

I dropped close to the ground, beside her.

"Just look, Alice. Isn't it great?"

The dill plants were a riot of gorgeous yellow flowers. Truly beautiful.

Renee whipped a tattered pamphlet out of the pocket of her jeans. "To paraphrase the bible," she said, holding the book up, "the leaves should be picked right after this little host of golden whatevers bursts forth."

I caught a glimpse of the cover of her "bible," a guide to herbs published by the Brooklyn Botanic Gardens. Like most writers, Renee loved to quote other writers—no matter what the subject, no matter what the context. She was very literate, like all of Barbara's friends. Except me—I just have an exceptional memory.

"But the plants look too lovely to touch," she continued. "How can I strip these poor flowers naked? I mean, it just seems a shame." She was clucking her tongue, half-joking, but only half.

I looked down at the plants, my mind not on them at all. I had other things to discuss right now.

"Listen, Renee," I began, turning to her. "Did Barbara ever talk to you about God?"

She frowned in answer, obviously not sure she'd heard me correctly.

"You mean . . . *God?*"

"Yes."

She stood then, and I stood along with her.

"What a bizarre question, Alice." There was a trace of a smile on her mouth, as if she thought I was making some sort of joke. "Why do you ask?" The smile disappeared as quickly as it had come.

"I don't know. Maybe I just want to flesh out my memories of her, complete the picture."

"I'm sure," she said deliberately, "I don't know what you mean by that, Alice." I knew then that I had upset her. "But isn't it a little soon to be making up things about her, mythologizing her? Isn't she fresh enough in your memory?''

I nodded apologetically and began to withdraw.

''Just a minute,'' Renee called to me, already back at work on the plants. ''The answer to your question is no. No God.''

''You mean for her or for you?'' I inquired.

She glared at me. What a madonna-like face Renee Lupo had, even when she was angry. She was one of those women who become more exotic as they age. Her hands, her neck, her feet—everything about her was precise and lovely and sculpted.

''Why don't you get to work like the rest of us?'' Renee asked.

''I will, shortly.''

''You're too full of yourself, Alice,'' she said.

''What do you mean by that?''

''What I mean by that is that you have an over-inflated view of your own thought processes.''

''I have good reason for asking the question I did, Renee.''

''Everybody has good reasons for stupid questions. Why ask any questions at all, Alice? Why not just mourn silently, like the rest of us? Why not just finish the garden?'' She seemed to be getting more and more hostile. She fiddled with the top buttons of her blouse, which now hung over the sides of her jeans. Her anger saddened me.

I walked over to the plant bed where Ava was working intently. She was, as usual, beautifully if inappropriately dressed beneath the gardening smock I recognize as one of Barbara's. Today's outfit was a soft ecru jumpsuit. Ava was a very handsome woman.

When she saw me she plucked a coriander leaf, then waited until I came close enough for her to thrust it under my nose. "Isn't it strange, Alice, that a plant with such wonderful seeds has such a vile-smelling leaf?"

No argument from me. The odor was indeed awful.

"Seeds aren't ripe yet," she added, turning the leaf over a couple of times before she let it fall to the ground. "Are you okay, sweetie? You look tired."

"I'm all right, thanks. Ava . . . ?"

"Yes?"

"How are the kittens?"

"Oh, they're quite wonderful. Quite mad. They run all day and all night. And in between they collapse. But never all at the same time. Winken runs. Blinken collapses. Nod watches. Then the cycle starts again. They're exhausting, but so much fun!"

I'd been stalling, of course, with that inquiry about the cats. It was time to be direct. "Ava, can you tell me if Barbara ever talked to you about religion, about God?"

She caught her breath then. A minute later she began to speak, but then could not. The tears started to roll down from her eyes. She said, "Oh, Alice. Do you know what Barbara was always talking about these last few months? You. She talked about you all the time. She was so taken with you, so happy about your friendship. She loved you . . ." And then Ava seemed to crumble from the sadness. She reached out for me and we stood holding each other.

I was two-for-two, as Basillio might say. So far

the inquiry had proved a fiasco. Renee was angry, Ava was desolate. This was not the way I'd planned it.

A few moments later, her tears dried, Ava left the plants temporarily to get a glass of water. I could see that Sylvia, too, had taken a break, and was standing at the fence, through which she was engaged in conversation with one of the neighbors who often came by to check on our progress.

When the conversation was finished and Sylvia had been left alone, I headed over to her. She was staring past me now, at the lonely-looking Ava.

Sylvia was still putting on weight, and her short-cut hair accentuated that fact. She was wearing the skirt to a spinsterly woman's suit, the kind Margaret Rutherford used to wear in the old Miss Marple films. As usual, she looked exhausted; maybe that was the price you paid for having an alcoholic husband who needed a lot of indulging. But Sylvia remained a very smart and kindly woman.

"What's the matter with Ava?" she asked, the concern evident in her voice.

"I'm afraid I upset her," I said, "with a question I asked about Barbara."

"What question?"

"One I planned to ask you as well," I said, feeling a bit sheepish, but determined to go through with it anyway. "I wanted to know if Barbara ever talked about religion; about, well, God."

Sylvia's reaction was certainly underplayed, compared to the others'. She smiled a little at me. "Grief is a strange thing," she said. "Faulkner said if there was a choice between Grief and Nothingness, he'd choose Grief."

"I don't think I understand what that means."

"I think it means one shouldn't kill oneself," she said wryly.

Sylvia reached down to retrieve her trowel from the ground. Then she said, "To answer your question, Barbara never spoke to me about God. But I remember talking to her about it—Him—once, in a way. A couple of years ago. Virginia was at the vet's for an operation and I was very worried about her. Barbara came over to spend some time with me. Pauly was away at the time. Anyway, when Barbara arrived she found me reading Simone Weil. Ever hear of her?"

I shook my head.

"She was a radical intellectual who starved herself to death out of allegiance with the . . . with all of suffering mankind. She wrote: 'Every time I think of the Crucifixion, I commit the sin of envy.' "

Sylvia paused to tap the trowel against the wire fence and shake off some caked earth.

"But Barbara," she continued, "didn't want to talk about Weil. All she said was that she knew absolutely that the cat was going to be all right. That I shouldn't worry."

She banged the trowel savagely then. "You know, sometimes I think we should just raze this stupid garden. I know Barbara would have wanted us to follow through, but it just makes no damn sense without her. None!"

The implement clanged back to the ground and I bent down to pick it up. Sylvia brought both her hands to her head and pushed backward along the sides, as if she had long hair that was in her way.

"Barbara *should* have talked about God," she said, "because she was the holiest person I ever met. She was, wasn't she? There wasn't one mean or spiteful or jealous bone in her body. She was selfless, you know? For instance, about five years ago Barbara and Tim were in big trouble financially. Now, I have more money than I know what to do with. And when I wanted to lend her—not lend, just give it to her—ten thousand dollars, she said no. She wouldn't accept it. But not out of pride. No. You know what she said? She said she was ready to be poor for a while, if that's how it was meant to be."

Sylvia shook her head and took the trowel back from me. "I'm going to get back to work now, Alice. Join me when you want to work up a sweat." She walked slowly back to the catnip.

This part of the investigation had been a study in miscalculation. If I continued in this way I'd manage to do the one thing I wanted most to avoid: alienate Barbara's best friends.

I turned my back on the garden and looked out at the street through the high fence.

There had to be a better way to proceed, I knew. A more logical way. Start at the beginning. Start with the person who had brought me those jogging clothes and set the whole thing in motion—Tim Roman. I didn't know why I hadn't thought of that first. Because Basillio had disappointed me? Rothwax had dismissed me? At least he had cautioned me against an investigation that proceeded from "feelings." But I had fallen into that trap anyway, foolishly, childishly.

We were all—all of Barbara's friends—like children in one respect, it seemed. We all wanted to

shut our eyes tight, then open them suddenly and
see Barbara standing there again.

But of course that would surprise the hell out of
the one who had killed her.

8

It was nine days later, and I had not yet phoned Tim Roman.

My visit to the herb garden to interrogate Barbara's closest friends had brought nothing but unhappiness. It had been a sobering, chastening experience, and had caused me to question all my convictions about Barbara's death. And now, as I lay all the facts and assumptions and unknowns out on the table, I knew I had very little. I was more and more inclined to let the dead stay dead.

In the nine-day interval, I got a new cat-sitting job. I was also called for an interview with an executive from one of the cable channels who was thinking of producing a three-part serial, à la *Masterpiece Theater,* about the doomed poet Sylvia Plath. He was considering me for one of the voiceovers; I'd be reading her poems over the live action. And one day was completely taken up with capturing Pancho and getting him to the vet to be treated for his pancreatic insufficiency.

Each time I'd picked up the phone to call Tim Roman, something had prevented me from completing the call. It was my conscience. The idea of prying into his and Barbara's life together, trying to trap him, was just too much to bear. I imagined putting the same question to him that I'd asked the women at the garden—"Did Barbara ever talk about God or religion?''—and the mere thought sent shivers down my spine. I could just see him dissolving with grief again, or maybe even flying into a rage at me. Even more terrible, I could envision myself telling him that Barbara had been deceiving him, that the jogging story had only been a cover for her planned conversion to Catholicism. And I hated all of it.

The bottom line was that I could not believe Tim had had anything to do with Barbara's death. So why put him through that?

And so the days passed and I went about the business of my life.

Basillio woke me at six-thirty on the morning of day number ten.

"Hey, Swede. Did I wake you?"

"Of course you did." I felt no obligation to disguise my irritation.

"Well, good," he responded. "You have to start being an early riser. It's the early bird that catches the criminal worm, you know."

I made no reply, deciding not to tell him about my early-morning reconstruction of Barbara Roman's routine. My silence did nothing to dissuade him from rattling on, however.

He was full of witty, self-deprecating comments about his exile in the Connecticut countryside. Then he said mysteriously, "Nan Molina sends her best to you."

I sat up in bed, still not totally awake. I tried to focus on the name, but it meant nothing to me. The line remained silent until he spoke again.

"Don't you remember Nan Molina?" he prompted cheerfully.

"It's six o'clock in the morning, Tony."

"It's six-thirty, but try to remember who Nan is."

"No."

"She wrote *The Vampire of Sixth Avenue!*"

Nan Molina and her play came back to me then. One of the more insane roles I had ever played, the heroine of *Vampire of Sixth Avenue* was a whimsical lady murderess who worked in one of those Sixth Avenue skyscrapers as a receptionist. By the end of the play she had disposed of twenty-one male bosses of all kinds. Actually a very funny farce, it even had music: an offstage harmonica player. The performances had been given in the basement of a Hispanic Pentacostal church on Upper Broadway.

I laughed at the memory.

"Ah, you *do* remember," Tony said.

"Yes, I do. Send her my regards."

"I don't like the way you sound, Swede."

"I'm not at my very best at this time of the day."

"That's not it, Swede. Are you still brooding over your friend's death? Not accepting it?"

"Perhaps I am."

"Well, leave it alone, Swede. Just stop it."

"Don't tell me what to do, Tony. The last time I sought your advice you were decidedly unhelpful. And why *are* you calling me at six in the morning?"

"Oh, I've been up all night with some of these idiot children. Actually, I'm just about to go to bed."

"Dear God. Grow up, Basillio."

"Uh, Swede?"

"What?"

"Do you mind if I make a pass at Nan Molina?"

"Let your conscience be your guide, Tony." I spoke much more softly than before.

He laughed. "You're sexy when you're annoyed, Swede. Call you again. Same time?"

I tried to get back to sleep after Tony's call, but it was no good. I lay there in bed, close to Bushy, who was snoring peacefully on the other pillow. There is only one window in my bedroom, high and narrow, and very little of the morning light had filtered in through it. The room was filled with shadows. I was—I couldn't deny it—depressed.

Too dispirited, for the moment, even to get up and make morning coffee, my thoughts kept on floating.

As for Basillio . . . well, I didn't know. My relationship with him was like one of those shadows. We irritated each other, we flirted, we made love, we parted and then came back together. The ground was constantly shifting beneath us. And just maybe he was seeking my permission for the Nan Molina pass a little bit *after* the fact?

No such confusion with Barbara. No shifting sands, no feuds, no condescension. I couldn't even conceive of Barbara's tearing off to another state to pursue some interest, and then having no time or patience for my concerns. We had had the best possible friendship, but it had been too short. Ended much too soon. I'd been cheated out of it.

While the coffee dripped, I called Tim.

He answered not with a "hello" but a "yes."

"Tim, this is Alice Nestleton." Not too businesslike, I hoped.

Nothing.

"Tim, are you there? I hope I'm not waking you." I glanced over at the clock. It was 7:40.

"No, you're not."

"How are you, Tim?"

"I'm okay. . . . Well, actually, I'm having a hard time working. Or thinking. I can't do much of anything except stare at the walls—and miss her."

At first I thought the labored breathing I was hearing must be Tim trying to rein in his emotions. Then I realized it was me. I started to mumble something in commiseration, but he kept talking.

"God, Alice. I can't stand the thought of her not existing anymore. I keep seeing her face in my head, falling, falling, and—"

I cut him off. "Listen, Tim, can we meet?"

"Of course. I want to talk to you."

"Yes," I said, "I want to talk to you, too."

"When?"

"Are you free tomorrow?"

"Tomorrow? Yes. Where shall we meet?"

"You pick the place, Tim. Wherever you like."

"There's a place on First Avenue. I never remember the name, but it's between Sixty-eighth and Sixty-ninth. On the east side of the street. It has a gray awning. We used to go there sometimes just to have a drink before dinner, just to sit and relax. I have an appointment midtown and can be there by three. How would that be?"

"Fine. I'll be there."

I hung up, momentarily choking on my own duplicity and bad faith. But I soon managed to swallow it down.

Something had taken Barbara away from me. Or someone had. As I said before, I'd been cheated.

But more important, so had Barbara. There and then I admitted to myself that I didn't give a damn if I had to hurt or alienate all of her friends and family. Maybe it was some lofty justice that I was after—or simple revenge. Or perhaps I was just a hostage to my own arrogance, my "feelings."

It didn't matter. In my own way, I was going to get her back.

9

Start to finish, it was one of the oddest days I have ever lived.

The morning seemed to go by in a blur. Make coffee. Feed cats. Newspaper. Suddenly it was afternoon. I felt inexplicably lightheaded. I found myself in front of the mirror, putting my hair up in a style that came out of nowhere—but I decided to leave it. I thought I saw Pancho do a kind of doubletake as I bent down to fill his bowl with dry food.

I'd discharged my cat-sitting duties by one-thirty, so I had all the time in the world to walk uptown to the bar where I was to meet Tim Roman. I stopped once to look at some brown suede shoes that had caught my eye, and once to buy a new lip rouge.

I kept reminding myself how important it was to keep focused. I wasn't out to hurt Tim, but I did need to extract information from him.

He had given me excellent directions. I had no trouble finding the place. Tim was the only person in the eating area. He pushed out his chair as soon as I entered the room. But as I walked toward him, I had the sensation that the man standing there smiling at me was a totally different man from the Tim Roman who'd been married to my friend Barbara. Different from the stunned and anguished man who'd brought me the jogging clothes and wanted me to talk to his orphaned cat.

He was dressed stunningly enough to be a full-page ad in the *Times* magazine. He was wearing an impeccably tailored gray suit with lighter gray pinstripes, an off-white shirt the color of which suggested the inside of a cucumber, and a rust-colored silk tie I recognized as a Hermes. He greeted me warmly, with a kiss on the cheek.

If my heart skipped a few beats before I returned his greeting, it was because . . . because, frankly, it had just hit me that Tim Roman was a beautiful man.

I felt a little under-dressed. I could only hope that my long black skirt and white cashmere V-neck sweater made me appear dramatic, rather than simply plain.

Something else was peculiar about this meeting. I'd never been in this bar before, but there was a familiarity about it. Not so much a real memory of it, as a theatrical one. As if I'd once walked onto a stage and made an entrance onto a set like this. As if I'd long ago sat with a man who looked like this, at a table that looked like this one. Maybe I'd lightly touched my pearl-and-jet necklace, as I was doing now, while we spoke. But the memory was a false one—I'd never been in such a play.

It was much more likely that Tim had sat here with Barbara on a hundred such occasions, that it was they who had been the "actors." She would come in, simply dressed but lovely, to meet her handsome husband. And the two of them would behave rather formally with each other, almost as if they were on a date. But how had all of this worked its way into my vault of memories?

"What would you like to drink?" Tim asked.

He was having some kind of whiskey, without ice, in a small glass. A tumbler of water rested next to his drink, untouched.

"A Bloody Mary."

He ordered the drink for me and another one for himself. (It was bourbon: Jim Beam.)

When my drink was placed before me, I took a fairly robust sip. "This tastes wonderful," I said. "I walked all the way up from Twenty-sixth Street, along First Avenue. I was thirsty."

"Long walk," he said, and I could see that he was admiring me, but not for the long walk. I caught that glance of his and held it for a while with my own.

And then the lady detective in me interceded.

"I passed the most charming little church on the way up here," I said. "Around Sixty-fifth Street. Do you know it?"

"No."

"A Catholic Church, but the signs announcing Mass and what-have-you are in Czechoslovakian— or Slovakian—or whatever they speak."

He went on looking at me, very still in his seat.

"This may sound like a strange thing to say," I went on, "but I just had the feeling that Barbara would have been quite taken with a little church like that . . . do you think?"

He shrugged. "Barbara never showed any interest in churches. We traveled all over Italy a few years ago. I don't think she visited a single one."

"Aren't they pretty hard to avoid in Italy?"

"No 'working' churches, I mean." He looked at me then with one of those shy, adolescent kind of smiles. Certain middle-aged men seem to have a patent on them. "But Barbara and I did go into

a church from the Middle Ages to see a few Ber-
nini's.''

''Was she an atheist?'' I asked. ''We never
really discussed things like that.''

''I wouldn't say that. It wasn't that she had anything against organized religion. She didn't care
one way or the other.'' Tim signaled the waiter
for another round of drinks.

Did he really believe what he'd just said? Obviously, Barbara had been very careful. But how,
really, was it possible for a woman to hide from
her husband the fact that she was taking formal
instructions in a religious faith? How could one
party in an intimate relationship hide from the
other a new—and perhaps profound—religious
belief? More to the point, *why?* Why had Barbara
been so secretive? Who would have objected—or
cared? I was sure that among her enlightened
friends the attitude must have been ''live and let
live.'' There were a lot worse passions than Catholicism.

Tim began to discuss the bar itself—not just how
much he and Barbara had liked it, but its neighborhood aspects. How long the place had been on
this spot; how it had once been located across the
street; who'd had a wedding reception here, and
so on. I listened to his easy, free-flowing narra-
tive, still struck by how *different* he seemed:
pulled-together, modulated, droll—and very beautiful.

We had fallen into a silence. But not an edgy
one. We were calm. At ease. He watched me as I
sipped my Bloody Mary through the straw. It was
mildly spicy, as I had requested.

After a bit he said: ''It is very nice sitting here
with you. Barbara would be pleased if she knew.''

How on earth could I respond to that? I didn't. "You know," I said instead, "I don't think I even know exactly what kind of designer you are."

"I design what you're sitting on."

Puzzled, I guessed, "Underwear?"

He laughed out loud—a large, nice laugh, familiar and hearty. "No. Chairs. You're drinking with the guy who won first prize for a three-legged rattan number. In Milan. 1984."

"I'm impressed. I never knew a chair designer before."

"And I never knew an actress with a passion for crime."

"Only when the client pays me," I lied. "Actually, my only remaining passions are for Maine coon cats and . . ." What was it I had almost said, "friends"?

"What about the herb garden?" he asked.

"That was Barbara's passion, not mine. She was the one who made everything work."

Tim picked up the theme. "She made everything work." Now I could see, in the corners of his countenance, traces of the fragile widower I'd come to know. So he *was* still precarious, probably prone to wild mood swings, sudden bouts of tearfulness, plunges into morbidity.

I looked in the direction of the three men at the bar, all of them watching a bike race on the cable TV sports channel. The digital clock near the set said it was 5:14. One by one, the bar stools were being claimed by after-work drinkers.

"I should get going," I said.

"No." Tim leaned forward and caught my hand. The anxiety in his voice betrayed the casual gesture. "No, don't go yet, Alice. Come with me and . . . say hello to Swampy."

Because he was my friend's husband . . . that must explain why I'd never noticed how wonderful-looking he was.

I found myself looking down at his perfectly formed knuckles. "I will," I said, "if you'll tell me the story of how you and Barbara first met."

"Why do you want to know that?"

"No reason. Because."

"And she never told you?"

"No, never."

"Then it's a deal. You can comfort Swampy, and I'll tell you how we met—for what it's worth. And I'll make you coffee, too. I make excellent coffee."

Five minutes later we were inside the roomy apartment. Tim went into the kitchen, which soon was filled with the racket made by an old coffee-grinder.

I started crooning to old Swampy, who lay stretched out on the rug, his massive alley-cat head cocked to one side as if the weight of it were too much for him. He acknowledged my presence with the merest glance.

The coffee seemed to be taking forever. As my conversation with Swampy was going nowhere, I got up and started to look around the apartment. I'd been here a few times before, but not very often. The place needed a paint job. And though much of the furniture was hand-me down, those pieces mixed in seamlessly with the various antique end tables and armchairs scattered around the huge living room. What was obviously not a particularly special or charming space had become so simply through the presence of the people who'd lived in it.

Here and there I saw an object that Barbara obviously had either hunted down or come upon and just had to have: a hand-carved tortoise from South America, a watercolor of a sea bird, an Egon Schiele print. In fact, I knew that if I looked carefully I would find her spiritual fingerprints all over the house. And even though she had died somewhere else—for a possible indiscretion that might have occurred somewhere else—I felt that the search should begin here in her home. Wasn't that really why I had agreed to come upstairs with Tim? At just that moment of awkward self-discovery, Swampy, draped over the back of the sofa, looked at me directly for the first time since I'd come in, and I could have sworn there was a hint of mocking laughter in his eyes.

Tim came in with the coffee then—in two tall, steaming mugs that seemed to have been carved out of onyx. He had removed his jacket but not his tie; his sleeves were rolled up to expose strong-boned wrists. We each sat on a straightbacked chair, separated by a small round table.

The coffee was really good, and I told him so. We sat drinking in silence for a few minutes more. I found myself wondering whether, if my best friend had been, say, Ava Fabrikant, I would be here in this strangely dreamy and morally ambiguous kind of situation with her husband Les. Hard to imagine it. What about Pauly, Sylvia's husband? Almost laughable. My reverie was broken by a query from Tim.

"What was it you asked? How I met Barbara?" I nodded.

He started to speak, but then stopped and looked over at Swampy.

"If you want to tell me," I added.

"Why wouldn't I want to?" he chuckled.

"There was nothing very mysterious about it." But again, he quickly stopped himself before he could begin the story. Tim put his cup down and started to remove his tie. When it was off, he folded it carefully and placed it on the table. His movements were catlike—effortless, but with a hint of violence. I never took my eyes off him.

"Know the criterion for a good chair design?" he asked, out of the blue.

"Does this have anything to do with how you met Barbara?"

"Probably. Most things have something to do with Barbara."

"Well then, no. I don't know the criterion."

"I mean, beyond beauty and function and durability of material. I mean the base, the real criterion."

"No," I repeated. "I do not know."

"It's simple. It's this: The person who uses a chair is supposed to feel better—mentally and physically—when he or she rises from that chair than when he or she sat down in it."

"That sounds . . ."

I saw Tim rising from his seat. He took the few steps over to my chair and then he was very close to me. "That sounds very logical," I said. His waist was at eye level, and I could see his rib cage moving beneath his shirt.

"Alice, I need your help," he said quietly, urgently, as he knelt in front of me.

"I will help you as much as I can, Tim."

He kissed me on the lips then, just for a second, but long enough.

"Do you know what it is to be frightened, Alice?"

"Of course I do."

He looked deep into my eyes. *"I'm* frightened, Alice."

"Of what?" I was speaking in a whisper now.

He placed his hand gently on the side of my head. "Of the next moment, and the next one after that, and the one after that. I'm frightened of a world that no longer makes sense to me."

And then his face was against my neck. He was speaking and kissing me with equal desperation. "I want to make love to you . . . in the bedroom. In the same bed where I used to make love to Barbara."

I took his face in both my hands, suddenly feeling desperate too. And horrible. I was seductress and seduced and victim and onlooker and villain and hero all at the same time—Barbara's avenger, Barbara's betrayer, Barbara's replacement.

"Come, Alice," he said, his voice strangely grave. "Don't you want to come into our room, my love?"

It made me feel beautiful, too, the way he looked at me, as if it were absolutely right, absolutely natural, to be here with him. I knew what Barbara must have felt every time he'd touched her in this way.

"Yes," I answered his question. And stood up, and accepted his long kiss, and took his hand, and walked with him into the room.

10

It had been a long time since a man spent all night in my bed. Bushy was confused and unhappy, having lost his pillow. He was stalking back and forth on the floor beside the bed, his tail raised. Pancho ignored the guest altogether, dashing from one end of the apartment to the other, just like always.

The sex had been overwhelming. I felt a solid joy in the fact that Barbara had selected this man for a husband, for he was a remarkable lover. *Now,* that is—I didn't know about the past. But who cared about the callow Tim Roman? Now he was the ideal middle-aged man. Slim and tall and strong and graceful and tender and intuitive and wise. He could be father, son, and lover all wrapped into one functional package.

Tim stretched languorously and smiled at Bushy. Then he pulled me close to him.

"How long ago was it when we first made love?" he asked.

"Three days."

"Seems much longer ago than that. Did you know what was going to happen when you came to the apartment?"

"Um-um," I said, fudging. I was lying and not lying. How could I know now what I had expected to happen three days ago?

"I want you to know I didn't have a master plan

to seduce you, Alice. I mean, I always liked you. I may have wondered what it would be like to be with you—if I weren't married—but I didn't know this would happen."

As we lay there, together, close, Barbara had never seemed more present.

I looked into that deep greenness of his eyes, for what seemed to be the millionth time. Tim was right—it did seem like ages ago that we first made love. Never before had I felt so comfortable with a man who was essentially a stranger. And with whom I had practically nothing in common— except, of course, our love for Barbara. Was he making love to me as a surrogate Barbara? Of course. But that wasn't the problem.

The problem was me. I seemed to have lost sight of everything important. I was bouncing off all the walls—suspecting Tim, deceiving him, sleeping with him; venerating Barbara, trying to avenge her, but at the same time trying to supplant her.

The confusion and conflict must have shown on my face. I heard Tim speaking to me as if he were far away. "What are you thinking about? Alice . . . ?" he whispered.

I moved away from his touch.

"Are you starting to feel a little guilty?" he asked. "Like we're betraying her in some way?"

"Barbara's dead," I replied softly. "You cannot betray the dead."

His face seemed to grow paler, the morning sun highlighting the strong lines running down each side of his jaw.

But of course I didn't believe a word of what I'd just said. One *can* betray the dead—feel love and anger and hate toward them. Or guilt. One can demand justice for the dead. That was why I had pursued Tim originally. And look at what had happened: I was now "involved" with Tim, to put it mildly. The truth was that my passion for him was total. And I no longer knew what I was doing.

It was then that I saw some of the old panic coming back into Tim's face. He suddenly sat up and began a disjointed kind of monologue.

"When it happened . . . Do you remember, Alice? We heard the sound of the cars, and then we looked down and saw that terrible thing on the road and then we looked at each other . . . and we realized that she was missing. Remember? What I felt then was so strange. It was as if Barbara were standing right beside me, but she was also down there, shattered, a heap of bones and flesh . . . dead. I was calm then. Because she took my hand. For some reason I recalled something I had read a long time ago. Some Austrian philosopher—I forget his name—said that the limits of your language are the limits of your world. That's what I was thinking as I stood there looking down. I knew I had reached the limit. Bang. The limit was like a wall. And I had hit it. And there was nothing to say. Nothing."

He went on talking. I watched his shoulders and chest rising and falling, as he spoke about how he could no longer really speak. About how Barbara's death had taken away his capacity for meaningful language.

I was watching his face closely. And in some disembodied way, I was watching myself watch him. I tuned in and out of his speech, which barely made sense. No, I didn't know what I was doing at all. Was all this—this tumble into intense passion—really about my desire to *be* Barbara Roman? My desire to be a woman whom others loved devotedly because I was wise and gentle and compassionate and capable? Perhaps I had leapt into Tim's bed, into his life, in exactly the same way I leapt into criminal cases. Did I just want to show others the truth they couldn't see? If I could show the police they were wrong about a case because they were looking through a glass darkly, then I guess I could show Tim Roman that I was another Barbara.

I snapped back into the present when I realized he was addressing me directly now. ". . . It's been so wonderful being with you," he was saying. "But sometimes I think you'll disappear, too. Afraid I'll touch you and you'll break into pieces."

"I won't," I said. "I'm not going to break."

He buried his face between my breasts.

I have to be careful, I thought. If I find myself needing him as much as he needs me, all my priorities will go out the window forever. Barbara's murder—if it was that—was supposed to be my first priority. I had to get to the point of looking at the affair with Tim as a gift—like finding a hundred-dollar bill in a used book.

We made love again, and again. And at last we lay side by side, neither touching nor speaking for a long time.

I had dozens of things to do that day: meet a new cat-sitting client, see my agent, do a laundry and a shopping, make some phone calls. But I just lay there.

"Alice . . ."

I touched him lightly on the thigh to signal that I was listening.

"I'm going to Atlanta tomorrow on business.

Could you . . . go up to the apartment and look in on Swampy?''

The request seemed so jarringly out of context, so ridiculously mundane, that I began to laugh uproariously. Then I got out of bed and went about the business of the day.

11

I entered the apartment whistling. The perplexities
aside, the past few days of lovemaking and inti-
macy with Tim had mellowed me greatly. My ob-
session with Barbara's death was receding with
every passing hour. I was in her apartment now
not as part of an investigation but merely to do a
favor for my lover.

I called out to Swampy, but he did not appear.
I even made a few of those clucking, kissy noises
that non-cat people always think win over a shy
cat. They never do, of course.

I then proceeded as if this were a standard cat-
sitting/apartment-check assignment: Water the
plants; make sure the windows are locked; clean
up the litter box; and so on. I peered into the bedroom, and for a moment was surprised to find the
bedcovers rumpled. Then I remembered that it was
Tim and I who'd done the rumpling.

There he was! Swampy was suddenly swaggering around after me in his threatening alley-cat
fashion. So I went to prepare his food according
to Tim's instructions: a little raw chopped veal and
a little raw chopped turkey from carefully labeled
containers in the refrigerator, topped off with some
plain yogurt and a dash of thinly chopped greens.
I must have done pretty well as chef, for Swampy

went at his food with relish. No alley cat on earth had it so good.

Then I walked into the living room, sat down on the sofa, and took out the two pieces of mail I had retrieved from my box just as I left my apartment.

One letter was an invitation to participate in a symposium on "The Future of the American Theater" at the august Yale Drama School. I laughed out loud, wondering if I was the only perpetually out-of-work actress who got invited to these things. Alice Nestleton, on the strength of a few critically acclaimed but obscure performances over a twenty-year span, had become some kind of cult figure. I've often thought that if I ever write my story it will be titled *How Stardom Eluded Me*. Maybe the theater somehow needed me to remain obscure. As Tony might say, "It's a dirty job, but somebody has to do it." I tore letter and envelope into four equal pieces.

The other letter was from—of all people—Tony Basillio. When I opened that envelope, a small piece of note paper attached to a newspaper clipping fell out.

He had scrawled on the note paper: "Now here's a *real* murder case. Solve this one." The clipping, from a Connecticut daily paper, read in part:

A shooting on the Merrit Parkway that left a college student dead apparently was triggered by a traffic dispute, police said yesterday, as they continued to search for the gunman who opened fire from a moving car. David Harrel of Darien, nineteen, was shot in the head early Sunday as he drove home with two friends after a night on the town in Manhattan. The shooting occurred at

about 4:30 A.M. in the northbound lanes of the
highway, when a dark-colored Volvo pulled
alongside Harrel's red Toyota pickup and four
shots were fired. Police said Harrel and his
friends, whose names were not released, had
been drinking in a bar on the Upper East Side of
Manhattan. Detectives said yesterday that Harrel
had cut off the Volvo on a ramp of the East River
Drive on the way home, and insults had been
exchanged. Both vehicles then proceeded
northbound at a high rate of speed for many
miles until the shooting occurred.

The clipping went on to tell more about the victim and give two phone numbers which anyone
who had information about the crime was asked
to call—all with a pledge of strict confidentiality.

Good old Basillio—half smart-aleck, half nurse-
maid. This was his not very subtle way of reminding me to desist in my inquiries about Barbara's
death. But I already had—more or less—desisted.
If it was suicide, I didn't know why. If it was
murder, I still didn't know why, or who. The inquiry was on hold because I was sleeping with
Barbara's husband.

Basillio's letter went into the trash as well. Finished with his meal, Swampy drifted into the room
looking doleful. I tried to make eye contact with
him, I cooed like a pigeon, I sang a little bit, but
he was having none of it. Finally I stuck my tongue
out at him. He was resolutely indifferent, but lov-
able nonetheless.

What could be sillier, I wondered, than a
middle-aged, lovestruck woman? "Love . . . thou
art absolute . . . sole lord of life and death."
Where was that line from? I watched for a few
minutes while the cat groomed himself vigorously.

Barbara had said that Swampy's tongue was raspy enough to take the polish off a shoe. As Swampy went on with his toilette, I felt that corrosive, inexorable wave of remorse begin to creep over me once again—I had Barbara's husband, I had her cat, and here I was, very much at home in her apartment. What next—her children? She had none. The pots and pans she cooked with? Her clothing?

That was another extraordinary thing about Barbara: She never really gave a damn about clothes. I'd seen her look ravishing in a thousand-dollar evening suit, but she looked equally beautiful in a thrift-shop jumper or gardening overalls.

When Swampy had finished with his cleaning ritual, he headed for the bedroom. Pulled along by my thoughts, I followed him.

There were two walk-in closets in the room. A his-and-hers setup I knew Tim had designed himself. And, yes, I opened her closet. The dresses and skirts and coats were arranged neatly on their hangers. There was a blouse I'd given her. On the floor of the closet the shoes were all lined up in sad little pairs. My invasion did not stop there. In the bottom drawer of the built-in dresser I saw her slips and panties and bras. Nestled in a corner of the same drawer was a pair of antique opera glasses in a red leather case.

Suddenly something flashed past me, so quickly and with such force that I let out a little cry.

It was Swampy, who had leapt into the drawer and was frantically scratching at something there.

"Swampy, you crazy cat! What are you doing?" I attempted to pull him out, but he was oblivious to me. In another second he had pulled from the pile of things a pale blue handkerchief. He jumped triumphantly from the drawer and onto the floor, his prey in his teeth. I bent down and snatched it from his jaws.

The handkerchief was silk and quite lovely, and had been folded to conceal something. No wonder Swampy had exhibited such enthusiasm: Nestling in the center was one of the packets of catnip from the herb garden.

But how had it gotten there? When we started the garden, we had all agreed not to bring home any catnip whatsoever to our own cats until the project was completed and we'd sold what we could. It was a good idea. The one person allowed to take the packets off the premises was me, and that was only because I was the salesperson. I had practically vowed on a stack of Bibles that neither Bushy nor Pancho would get so much as a sniff until the other cats got theirs.

Stranger still, this was one of the newer packets, the ones made up after Barbara's death. These had no price penciled in on the labels; that way, we figured the stores would have more leeway to charge whatever they wanted, which would make it easier to sell them.

I kept the little cheesecloth packet in one hand, and with the other held up the hankie to read the decorative monogram on its edge: RAL.

I realized then, to my tremendous annoyance, that I did not know Renee Lupo's middle name.

Why on earth would Renee have smuggled catnip from the garden crop and made a secret gift of it to Tim?

At my feet, Swampy was fairly snarling with anger and impatience. I'd stolen something from him. But Renee was a thief, too.

Why on earth? Why Renee? Why Tim?

12

I couldn't sleep.

For the past few nights I had felt I couldn't sleep without Tim next to me. Now I couldn't sleep—period. All through the day that blue handkerchief had been in my thoughts.

Basillio's standard words of caution kept coming back to me: "Go slow, Swede. Let's lay it all out before we jump any guns. Right?"

Right. All I'd found was a bag of catnip, gift-wrapped, so to speak, in a pretty handkerchief that might belong to Renee Lupo. Well, that wasn't quite the sum total of what I'd found. Before I left Tim's apartment, I'd looked in the file where Barbara kept all her papers relating to the garden.

One of the insurance documents, which contained all our names, revealed that Renee's middle name was Abra.

Although I was sleepless and worried, I thought I was being hyper-logical. If Tim could turn to one of Barbara's good friends—me—for "comfort," then why not another—Renee?

It was a big leap, I knew, but the logic could be taken a lot further. Tim was a complex, handsome, sexy man—right? He and Barbara may have had a good marriage, but there'd been room in it for her to keep some pretty big secrets from him—

right? So it stands to reason that he might have been keeping a few from her—right? Like an affair with Renee—right?

Suppose Tim and Renee had been long-term lovers . . . who figured it was time to kill Barbara. Logic can assume some strange shapes, but could it stretch as far as that?

What would Basillio say if he could hear me now? I would come in for all kinds of ridicule. I'd be a naïf who couldn't accept the fact that she was not her lover's only lover. He would recommend a long rest at a home for the thinking-impaired. And maybe he'd be right. Maybe I was making the same kind of mountain out of this molehill as I had done with my conviction that Barbara had been murdered.

Yes, Renee had been standing right next to me when we heard Ava's terrible scream. On the other hand, I had no idea where Tim was when Barbara drifted out onto the terrace. . . .

I went into the kitchen and opened the refrigerator. What I yearned for was fresh, raw milk like we used to drink on my grandmother's farm: thick and warm and grassy. Of course, the only thing I had on hand was a half-filled container of the low-fat pasteurized stuff. I slammed the door shut and went into the living room to pick up my script for the upcoming radio play I was to perform in.

All these crazy speculations were probably just more manifestations of my discomfort and guilt over the affair with Tim. Why had I allowed myself to get into such a situation? What was wrong with me? I opened the script and read the first passage my eye came to rest on.

ELECTRA: Then I will speak now. You say that
you have murdered my father. What confession
could heap deeper shame on you than that,
whether the act was just or not? But I must
reveal to you that your act was not just. No! You
were led to it by the wooing of that base man
who is now your husband.

I was playing Clytemnestra in this production,
mother of Elektra, and in a speech previous to this
one I have just confessed to her that indeed I had
murdered her father.

Had I been wooed? Had Tim wooed me as an
"assignment," on someone else's "orders"? Perhaps after I'd questioned Renee and the others
about Barbara's religious beliefs?

Among my many mistakes, I thought, was my
search for a secret life being lived by Barbara.
What about *Tim's* secret life? The fact that we were
lovers now would complicate matters, but there
were a few facts about Tim I simply had to un-
cover. There was no way for me to go on with him
while I had all these suspicions and doubts.

I thought of one possible way I could check on
Tim without his knowing—a vaguely dishonorable
way. I could contact Rothwax. I had been a RE-
TRO consultant for long enough to know that their
computer has the capacity to search a thousand
accessible databases in the city. All it needs is a
name and address and it can get into the motor
vehicles database, the courts, the hospitals. If a
person has ever bought a car, rented an apartment,
filed a lawsuit, stayed at a city hospital, paid a fine
to any municipal agency, contested a tax bill, been
arrested or mentioned in a newspaper report, applied for a license of any kind—the RETRO com-

puter can find the record, expand on it, cross-reference it, and spit out more personal information than one could possibly imagine.

Dishonorable . . . So be it. I dialed Rothwax's home number. The phone rang many times before a dazed voice answered.

"Who is this?!"

"Alice Nestleton."

There was no response for a minute.

"Detective Rothwax, are you there? I could use a favor from you."

The voice on the other end of the line exploded: "Damn it! It's one-thirty in the morning!"

I honestly had lost track of the time, and was terribly embarrassed to be reminded of my oversight. But I forged ahead. "Listen, I'm really sorry about the time. But I need a RETRO computer search."

"No way."

"Please don't say no. Couldn't you go in a little early and run it for me? No one would have to know."

"Too much to ask."

"But it's important. Please."

"This have anything to do with your friend who jumped?"

"She didn't— Yes. I need a profile on her husband."

"Why? Is he your number-one suspect now?"

I hesitated. "I didn't say that. But I . . . I don't quite . . . trust him. I need the profile."

"And . . . ?"

"What do you mean, 'and'?"

Rothwax was very smart. He'd picked up something in my voice.

"I mean, do we have something else working here—like a domestic squabble? A payback?"

"Detective, please!" I snapped. "If you'll just help me on this, I'll never ask for anything like this again."

"Damn right, you won't," he grumbled, then exhaled an audible sigh. He was going to agree to it. I gave him the particulars on Tim Roman.

"This won't come cheap, Cat Woman," he said at last. "It's going to cost you three drinks and a club sandwich." And then he hung up.

Elektra probably had been putting audiences to sleep for generations, but not me. It was three-thirty in the morning, and I'd read as much of the script as my mind could hold for the present. I had some yogurt, then turned to the depressing psychiatry text I'd picked up in a used-book store shortly after Barbara's plunge from the terrace.

The forbidding-looking doctor who'd written it said that health workers and relatives should be able to recognize which patients are legitimate suicide risks. I had circled the three major criteria:

—a sense of aloneness
—self-contempt
—murderous rage.

I couldn't think of any three traits that sounded *less* like Barbara Roman.

At last my eyes grew heavy. I fell asleep on the sofa.

The telephone rang at about eight-thirty. I snatched up the receiver on the first ring.

"Hi!" the friendly voice said.

It was Tim. "Alice, it's me."

"Yes, Tim. Hello."

"I'm home," he announced happily. "Alice, you okay?"

"Yes. How was the trip?"

"Fine. When can I see you?"

I tried to remember what city he'd been in—was it Albany, or Atlanta? I couldn't help wondering whether he was calling me before or after he'd called Renee.

"Not today, Tim," I finally said. "I think I've got a little flu or something. I'm not feeling very well."

"Have you called the doctor? I'll come over and nurse you."

"No, no. It's all right. Let me call you tomorrow. I'll see how I'm feeling then."

"Are you sure?"

"Yes. Um . . . Tim?"

"What?"

"Nothing. It's just . . . We've all been concerned about you, that you're doing okay. Everyone at the garden, I mean. Renee and I were talking about you just the other day. She sends her love."

There was silence on the line for a brief moment. And then he said, "Well, thanks. You take care of yourself."

I was on my second cup of coffee when the phone rang again. When I picked it up I heard: "Claire? It's me. I—"

I interrupted the caller. "This isn't Claire. You have the wrong number."

But the male voice insisted. "It's *me,* Claire. I've located a few of those items for you."

It was Rothwax, I realized then, not using my name because he was calling from the RETRO office.

"When can I pick them up?" I asked conspiratorially.

"This afternoon. I have to be uptown about three-thirty. Meet me at the bar on Seventy-second, west of Columbus, north side of the street. Okay, Claire?"

"Okay, Marmaduke," I said.

Should I be feeling acquitted or condemned? I knew Rothwax wouldn't have called so promptly unless he'd found something significant.

13

"Claire, I like my women to show up early. I like to see them waiting for me."

I took the empty barstool next to Detective Rothwax. "Well, I'm not early," I said. "I'm merely on time. And you're not calling me from RETRO now—my name is not Claire!"

"Why so snappy, Cat Lady? I'm the one who took the big risk."

"I'm sorry, Detective. I didn't sleep well, and my nerves are a little frayed."

This had to be the darkest bar I'd ever been in. But it was hardly anyone's idea of a romantic hideaway. From some faraway corner, a static-filled radio droned.

"Why don't we take care of first things first?" Rothwax said. "What are you drinking?"

"I don't know. Nothing heavy. A bottle of ale might be nice."

"No bottled ale here," he said.

"Whatever they have then."

When my stein of beer arrived I noticed that it had practically no foam. It smelled a little stale and looked a little thick. But I didn't complain. As I don't like beer, and knew I would only have a few sips, it made no difference.

"You don't look very comfortable," Rothwax

observed. "Maybe this place is a little too down-scale?"

I noticed the smirk on his face, but I let the comment pass. Apparently, Detective Rothwax was incapable of passing up any opportunity to tweak me.

"I prefer to think of this place not as seedy but . . . what? . . . *mysterious*. Know what I mean? And besides, you seem like the kind of actress who could get into studying the down-and-outs."

I sipped my drink and asked, in a calm tone of voice: "Do you have something for me, Marmaduke?"

He turned on his seat to face me then. "Yeah, I do. But I just want to ask you one thing first."

"Which is?"

"Is this Roman guy your number one—in addition to being your number-one suspect?"

"I have no intention of discussing that with you," I said, more prissily than I'd intended.

His laugh was short and dirty. "Watch your step, Alice. That's not very professional."

I attempted to say something else to put him in his place, but he cut me off and launched into his report.

"First of all, your number-one friend—the bereaved—filed a divorce action two years ago. But it was never executed. I don't know why. Anyway, the action was withdrawn."

I sat up very straight.

"I take it you didn't know that?" he said.

I shook my head, silent.

"Ready for fact number two?"

"Go on," I said.

"Mr. Roman uses a mail drop."

"What's a mail drop? Something like a post office box?"

"Sort of. Let me explain it to you." He said that as though my ignorance of these matters was some sort of moral failing. "Okay. You're a cat-sitter, right? Imagine that you want to expand your business. You put an ad in the paper. But you don't want to use your real name for some reason, and you don't want all the replies coming to your apartment. So you go downtown to the city clerk's office. There, you file a paper that says from now on you'll be doing business in New York as the Bombay Cat Company. You pay a fee to do business in the city and you get a certificate and a tax number. Now you take the tax certificate to a place that is going to be your mail drop—say, 507 Fifth Avenue. You show them the certificate and pay another small fee up front and agree to a monthly charge of twenty bucks, and you can receive as much mail for the Bombay Cat Company as the suckers—customers—want to send. And you get a listing in the lobby. All you have to do is show up every few days and collect your mail."

"And Tim Roman does that?" I asked, not sure how all this nonsense applied to Tim.

"Right. He has a mail drop at 500 Fifth Avenue under the name of Oak Tree Designs."

"Well that makes sense, I suppose. He *is* a furniture designer."

"I guess. But there's a complicating factor."

"What's that?"

"This company name he uses, 'Oak Tree,' which isn't really a company at all, just a mail drop, leases an apartment." Rothwax smiled again. "Just stop me if I'm telling you anything that you already know."

"I don't know of any apartment other than the one he lives in—lived in with his wife."

"Well, this one is in the Village. A walk-up on Bedford Street, which is a couple of blocks east of Hudson."

One surprise after another. Tim was full of them. I felt a little sick. I copied down the address Rothwax gave me, and then asked, "How long has he had this place?"

"Six years."

I calculated the odds of Barbara's having known about that apartment. I calculated the odds that Tim and Renee had been lovers for all those years. The odds that all Tim and Barbara's friends had been hoodwinked into believing they'd had a wonderful, serene, trusting, ideal marriage.

"Was any of that helpful, Cat Woman?"

"Very much so, Detective. Very much so."

"Always happy to help a lady open a can of worms, you know. Now, how about another drink?"

I shook my head.

As Detective Rothwax inhaled his sandwich, I thought back to that last evening of Barbara's life, when Renee had told us about trap-gardening: You trap garden pests by luring them away from their primary goal. I decided to do a little trapping of my own.

14

Ava was throwing a tantrum in the peppermint patch. We were all in the herb garden, along with three neighborhood children who were garden helpers.

Ava was holding something up and yelling out: "I know these things are killing the peppermint. I know these ugly creatures are going to destroy the whole garden before we get it all harvested. I know it! I know it! I know it!"

Renee, Sylvia, and I stood gaping at the small object in Ava's hand. It appeared to be some kind of worm or slug—white and undulating.

"I *must* know what this is. I have to know!" Ava cried out.

"It's Uncle Wiggly," Sylvia commented wryly, "tunneling his way to Connecticut."

Ava shot a furious glance her way.

Returning to her own work, Renee called over her shoulder, "Kill the bloody thing."

As she said it I looked closely at her dark, lovely face. *Kill the bloody thing.* The words had a certain ugly resonance. Could she have pronounced Barbara's fate in that same cold-blooded, matter-of-fact voice?

Dark women threw me, particularly if they were intense—and Renee certainly was that. Since childhood I had had that old romantic nonsense rooted in my head that light-haired women could be ice maidens or bubbleheads, but dark women knew the secret things—the things that count. Growing in me now was a radiating rage toward Renee and her lover. But with that rage, confusion. Why was Tim sleeping with both of us? Why had he started up with me? Did Renee know? And had Barbara known about Renee?

"Where there's one, there are many more," Ava was still raving. "They're down there right now, destroying." Then she flung the wriggling slug away, as hard as she could, but because it was so small we couldn't see where it landed.

"You're the one who's always quoting those dumb horticultural books you read." Ava hurled those hostile words in Renee's direction. "Why can't you tell us how to get rid of these horrible, slimy creatures?"

It was odd how all of this animosity had surfaced so suddenly. The ghost of Barbara's love was definitely not hovering about the garden today. The four of us were like the survivors of some horrible accident, trying to forget what had brought us all together in the first place. Without Barbara, it was becoming painfully clear how little the rest of us had in common.

"Listen, dear," Renee was saying carefully, trying to defuse Ava's anger. "Peppermint is very hardy. The books say it's plagued by very few pests. Besides, when it was introduced here after the Civil War—"

"But peppermint *is* American," Ava cut in haughtily.

"Hardly," Renee shot back. "It most likely originated in Hindustan, and then was carried to Egypt, and from there to England."

"You know so much," Ava said bitterly, "but you can't even identify a worm that's going to kill all our plants."

That's when I stepped in. I shouted at the top of my lungs, as if to call time-out before a game broke into fistfights.

"We are all tired and on edge! I am declaring an official break! I want you all to come to my apartment for lunch today!"

There were no takers at first. Everyone had an appointment, a duty, a headache. But I wore them down.

"Just for an hour or so. Come at twelve-thirty. We'll be done by two. I think it's a good idea to meet in another setting once in a while. We're at each other's throats today. And we're supposed to be friends. After all, didn't we decide to finish what we started here at the garden because of our friendship with Barbara?"

They hesitated, looking sheepishly at one another. I watched Renee's face. She was the key. The trap had been set just for her. I wanted to find out once and for all if she and Tim had been, or continued to be, lovers. And whether they'd been responsible, in any way, for Barbara's death.

"Well," Sylvia finally said, "it's fine with me. But don't go to any trouble, Alice. It's too warm to eat, anyway."

"Yes," Ava agreed. "I'd love to meet Bushy, though." She smiled. "Barbara told so many funny stories about him."

Renee looked at me strangely; almost slyly, I thought. I couldn't tell whether she suspected that I was up to something. "It's very kind of you, Alice," she said. "Of course we'll come."

I noticed the grin on Sylvia's face then. She was

looking and pointing to the far side of the garden, where one of the neighborhood children, hardly more than a toddler, was helping another with the weeding of the basil.

"Isn't that divine?" she cooed. "Imagine how happy it would have made her to see that."

At least I was leaving them all in a more agreeable mood—for the moment, anyway.

I headed for the cheese shop on Second Avenue. Waiting in line, I saw a tall man who reminded me of Tim. An awful thought came to me: What if Tim called or—far worse—decided to drop in while all the ladies were lunching? We'd have the makings of a real drawing room farce then. Or the closing scene in a Charlie Chan movie.

I made a couple of other quick purchases—fresh berries, water biscuits, real cream—and by the time I'd reached Twenty-third Street I had everything I needed except the pastries. Those I would obtain in the chi-chi patisserie around the corner from my place.

But when I walked through the door and saw the dazzling array of goodies, I was hit by a sudden and paralyzing loss of will. I simply didn't know what to get. I stood in front of the counter for the longest time. Then it became clear: For the moment, I was my Gram. My grandmother was a strong woman who had run a Minnesota dairy farm all by herself. She was plain and tough, but she also had her own aesthetic. And she would have been appalled by the ostentation and overkill of a place like this. She might have accepted a choice between white bread and black bread, but a third or fourth choice would have struck her as being the height of frivolity.

Having gained a new perspective on the matter

by becoming my Gram for a moment, I quickly selected four raspberry tarts and one kiwi from the tray that the smiling young woman behind the counter was holding up for me. She boxed and tied them with a flourish, then sent me on my way with a cheerful ''Bon appetit!'' The truth was, I wasn't my Gram! I appreciated the good things of life too much for that.

Out I strode, to cover the final block to my place. I hadn't gone three steps before I realized what I'd just done. I'd purchased five tarts, when there would only be four for lunch. The fifth was unlike the others, and I'd bought it for Barbara.

At that moment I knew I *had* to solve the mystery of Barbara's death, justice and revenge and ego and jealousy and all else aside. Because if I didn't do that soon, I was going to go all the way around the bend.

15

I could hear them laughing as they made their way slowly up the stairs. They were three wealthy women. Every one of them lived in a building with an elevator. I could tell from their voices that the climb up to my apartment both tired and amused them. It was a kind of adventuresome slumming—like going to a play in an out-of-the-way loft.

They were all a little breathless when I admitted them. All still dressed in their gardening duds, three elegant farmers on a coffee break.

I gave them each a tall glass of iced coffee to refresh them.

"Oh, dear," Ava exclaimed, looking ruefully down at her three-hundred-dollar boots. "We should have taken our shoes off. I'll bet there's loads of dirt from the garden we're tracking all over Alice's home."

"Don't worry," I said. "I'm under no illusion that this is a Japanese restaurant. And besides, even actresses own vacuum cleaners."

They laughed at that, but it was really Sylvia who set the tone for the luncheon. "I'm so glad you asked us over for this little repast, Alice. You were right—we needed to get out of the garden for a bit. And I for one flatly refuse to discuss anything pertaining to that place this afternoon. Not fertilizer, not worms, not how many packets sold. Not anything!''

She was roundly applauded.

"What a beautiful table!" Ava had strode over to my long table, which stood against the far wall and which was now laden with goodies.

Sylvia and Renee followed suit, their hands and eyes running over the table. It was the only piece of real furniture in my apartment. The other pieces amounted to little more than a grab bag assembled over the years by a perpetually out-of-work actress who used to move every time the lease was up and sometimes before.

But this table had been my grandmother's. And it was the only large memento of her life and times on the dairy farm that I still had.

She had used it as a kitchen table. It was well over two hundred years old, and originally had come from France. Gram had bought it at an auction when she was first married. The table was made of cherry wood, and it was so tough it probably could withstand a nuclear attack. There were sliding drawers and planks all around the sides.

"It was my grandmother's," I told Ava, "and the only thing I have left from her farm."

"Look," Renee said, running her hand over old circular scars near the far end of the table. "Your grandmother must have put up a lot of fruit."

I smiled at her. It was strange to hear a sophisticated urban writer using "put up"—the country term for canning and preserving.

"My grandmother," I replied, "turned canning into an art form. She used to consider color and shape as well as function. She would can green beans with two flawless rows on top of each other. And she would get the pickles exactly the same size and lay them in two rows around the pint jar. And beets? She would preserve the juice to keep the dark color, and she would get all the little beets the same size. She used to warn me that when I grew up and started to put up cooked beets, I must remember to leave the stem in or they'd bleed to death and turn white.''

''I would have liked to meet and talk to your grandmother,'' Ava said wistfully.

For some reason I was caught up in a flood of canning memories. I could see her working. I could see her in that massive, always cold farm kitchen, the house cats watching her. I wanted suddenly to tell my visitors everything I remembered.

''Peaches were her specialty. She was very careful with them. She would skin them, and lay them on top of each other right up to the top to make the jar look elegant. She always lined the lids up. The Ball on the lid with the Ball on the jar. Or the Kerr with the Kerr. In those days she couldn't just go out and buy new ones. She used the same jars for years.''

''Still a country girl, aren't you, Alice?'' Ava asked approvingly.

No. I was no longer a country girl. I no longer froze every night of the long Minnesota winter. I no longer cut my fingers in freezing slush taking care of the dairy cows. But I couldn't stop talking for the moment.

''And she made a relish. A wonderful relish. Every year. It was called piccalilli. She made it with green tomatoes and red and green peppers and onions and cabbage.''

I could smell it again: sweet and sour, pungent and beautiful.

"And she was a wizard with jelly. Wild plum and wild strawberry jelly. She hated any strawberries but the wild kind. She wouldn't eat domestic strawberries. She wouldn't even taste one."

It suddenly dawned on me that I was beginning to talk to my three visitors in the same nonstop, revelatory manner I used to use when talking to Barbara alone. That realization made me feel uncomfortable. It was inappropriate. They were not in my apartment to hear my revelations. They were here because I had set a trap, because I was hoping they would reveal themselves.

I decided to keep my mouth closed and take the group on the ten-cent tour of my apartment. I walked them out of the living room and down the long hallway, past the closets and the kitchen, and through my bedroom at the end of the hall and the large, old-fashioned bathroom next to it.

That finished, we made our way back to the living room and started in on the cheese and crackers. In a few minutes Bushy wandered in, and they all focused their attention on him, resplendent as only coon cats can be. They petted him and oohed and aahed and he ate it up.

When he tired of the adoration and walked majestically away, I set my plan in motion. We were having a genuinely good time, but I had to do it.

I waited for a momentary lull in the conversation, then began solemnly, confidentially: "I want to talk for a few minutes about something having to do with Barbara."

At the sound of her name, the whole atmosphere changed. All eyes turned to me. Renee paused in slicing a piece of Stilton; Sylvia regarded me grimly through half-closed eyes; and Ava seemed to throw her head back in a defiant gesture, as if challenging me to continue.

Which I did. "Tim Roman," I said, "has given me some things to remember her by. I'm sure you've all received some mementos as well."

There were nods all around.

"He gave me her carnelian bracelet," Ava volunteered.

"I was given a lovely old cedar chest," I lied, "which was very thoughtful of Tim. But the strange thing was what I found inside of it."

"What?" Sylvia asked, and both the others leaned forward to hear my answer.

"A package of letters."

"What letters?" That was Renee.

"Letters written to me. Written to me by Barbara." I paused for maximum effect. "Sealed, and addressed, but never sent. I don't even know, in fact, whether Tim knew they were there. I found them under a flap at the bottom of the trunk."

"But why would she do that?" Sylvia asked. "Why write them and not mail them? What did they say?"

"Well, that's the thing, you see. I don't really know what they say."

"What do you mean, you don't know?!" She was incredulous. "Didn't you *read* them?"

"No, I haven't opened them. Oh, I've started to—a hundred times. But somehow I can't. It's as though they're her private thoughts, even though they're addressed to me. The thing is that she never actually sent them to me. So it's almost as though they aren't really meant for me to read. Do you understand?"

"I most certainly do *not* understand, Alice," Ava answered. "It's preposterous."

"It's macabre," Sylvia said.

"It's ridiculous," Renee said. "And I'd like to know why you're making this more melodramatic than it has to be. Why *shouldn't* you look at them? Why shouldn't we *all* know what's in them?"

"You will," I said. "I promise you will—but not right away. I thought I'd keep them, sealed, just the way they are, for a year. And then, on the anniversary of her death, next year, I'll open them and read them all . . . and so will all of you. We'll get together expressly for that purpose. Right here."

"Well, they are *your* letters. But I think it's one of the most ridiculous things I've ever heard," Renee said huffily.

"Dear God," Ava exhaled. "You certainly do know how to manipulate an audience, Miss Actress Nestleton. I could use a drink."

I went to fetch a gin and tonic for her. As I was leaving to do so, I heard Renee excuse herself to the others.

As I served the drink, Sylvia asked to see my clippings from the old days. Barbara had told her, she said, that I'd been the brightest of stars at the Guthrie. I located the scrapbook and handed it to her to share with Ava.

Down the hall, I could hear Renee making a big deal of running the water in the sink, then making much too much noise closing the bathroom door. I waited for her to join us again, and after a minute slipped out of the room myself and headed for my bedroom.

The trunk—which actually had belonged to my mother—was on the far wall of the bedroom. My scheme for rigging it came right out of pulp detective fiction. A small piece of fabric attached from the inside would be dislodged if anyone opened the trunk. The cloth was so small, in fact, that no one would notice it falling to the floor—especially if the lights weren't on.

As I checked out the trunk, I saw quite clearly that Renee had taken the bait. Both little piles of clothing I'd put in the chest were slightly rumpled from her search for the nonexistent letters. I hastily replaced the fabric inside.

This seemed to offer fairly solid proof of the Tim–Renee connection, but I had a long way to go before I could prove murder.

From the hallway, I listened to everyone's comments as they pored over the scrapbook. I called to them that I'd rejoin them as soon as I made fresh coffee. In a few minutes, Ava joined me in the kitchen.

"We're all dying to meet Pancho," she said. "Where is the dear old loon?"

"I'll try and run him to ground," I replied. "You keep an eye on the coffee."

I went back into the bedroom and called out to Pancho, sure he was in his favorite hiding place: a shoebox under the bed. I told him some fans were waiting to see his flying act, but he didn't appear. He could have been any one of a dozen places, though—in back of the stereo, or behind one of the high kitchen cabinets, or up on a shelf in the broom closet. At any rate I was tired of calling him, down on all fours and talking into the darkness under the mattress. As I started to rise, I caught sight of the little piece of fabric on the floor—where it had drifted, obviously, when someone else opened the trunk.

More than likely, Ava had been the second intruder. Just before she'd come into the kitchen to ask about Pancho.

"No sign anywhere of Pancho the Weird," I said as I rejoined the group. "You'll have to forgive his bad manners."

I looked from Renee to Ava, and back again. They both smiled innocently.

"Maybe you have a photograph of him?" Renee suggested.

"Sorry."

"Is he as crazy as Swampy?" Ava asked.

"Oh," I said, "Pancho is a full-blown psychotic. Swampy just seems to be an eccentric alley cat."

"And a very lonely one," Renee added.

Suddenly the cup in Sylvia's hand began to rattle.

"Darling, what's the matter!" Ava rushed to her side. Sylvia had grown pale.

"Nothing to worry about," Sylvia replied wearily. "No, please don't fuss. It's only my blood pressure." She leaned back and tried to breathe evenly. "All I need is one of my pills and a little lie-down. Just ten minutes."

Renee and I helped her into my room. I wet a cloth and placed it on Sylvia's forehead.

Renee said, "She'll be okay, really. I've seen this happen to her before. Just give her a couple of minutes."

Renee *and* Ava wanted to help with the dishes. Their presence, the two so close to me in the small kitchen, made me terribly uncomfortable. It was as if we were all in Tim Roman's bed together.

I left them putting away the plates and went down the hall to check on Sylvia. She didn't hear me open the door. Somehow, it was not an overwhelming surprise to find the bed empty and to see her bent over the chest, frantically going through the things in it. I stepped back out into the hall, and after waiting a minute or so, I knocked.

After she'd rejoined the rest of the group in the living room, she told us that she felt "tons" better and could make it down the stairs just fine under her own steam.

And so ended my brilliantly conceived luncheon! If I thought Renee's search for the letters proved an affair between her and Tim, then I had also just proved that Tim was sleeping with every single one of us.

Perhaps my guests had all been foolish to swallow that bizarre story about un-sent letters. But none was a bigger fool than I.

Seconds after the door had closed behind my luncheon guests, Pancho made a kamikaze leap from somewhere, landing on my old scrapbook.

While I vacuumed, I ate Barbara's kiwi tart.

16

I woke suddenly, not knowing where I was—one of those strange black panics that seem to come with greater frequency as one grows older.

I remembered cleaning up after my garden co-workers had left. And then lying down for a nap. I'd slept for almost five hours—in my clothes.

Okay. I was completely awake now. My name was Alice, and I'd made an ass of myself earlier in the day. The "trap" I'd laid earlier in the day had been a disaster. I had to try to clear my head and formulate another plan.

I threw a couple of things into a bag. No, I wasn't running away from home, from all my problems. I needed a swim. A friend of mine—an actor who'd made it big in daytime television—lived in one of the fancy high-rises on the East River. She'd arranged it that I could use the roof-top pool and sauna any time of the day or night.

As I piled up the laps I won a gold medal, at least in my own imagination.

I left the pool invigorated and hungry—but void of ideas, except about dinner. A few stars were out. I meandered toward the apartment until it occurred to me that the supermarket would be closing momentarily. I quickened my pace, at the same time making a mental shopping list. The cats' larder was pretty well stocked, but I had very little in the kitchen. I needed coffee, sugar, dish soap, paper towels, spinach, potatoes, juice, ground beef—the list grew as I trotted along. Oh yes, and candles.

Now, why did I need candles? Was I expecting a blackout? Did I mean to light one for Barbara? There must be an apt Chinese proverb for this stupid state of affairs. Something about faithless husbands. Light a candle for every woman your husband has slept with . . . and then call the fire department. We couldn't *all* be Tim's lovers, could we? That was absurd—not impossible, just absurd.

The narrow aisles of the market are dangerous at that time of evening. Everyone's in a frantic rush to finish their shopping before closing time, blindly spearing items from the shelves. I'm one of the worst offenders. I behave like an Amazon warrior when I reach the paper goods section. My final catch totaled sixteen items, so I could not use the express line. Needless to say, it took longer to get checked out than to do the actual gathering of the items.

It was a beautiful night—breezy and black and velvety—and the streets had taken on that eight o'clock kind of glamour. I didn't notice him until I was right at my doorstep.

"Tony!"

Basillio greeted me then reached out to help me with my package.

"What happened, Basillio? They fire you because of that smart mouth of yours?"

"Swede," he said, a little sadly, "ever since I was a kid I've really deep-down hated *Julius Caesar*. I mean, when I was nine I memorized Mark Antony's funeral oration. And I was as impressed by Brando as the next guy. But now I find myself in some godforsaken part of *Connecticut,* listening to some awesome hunk from Purdue spieling the same lines. . . . I needed a day off, Swede. Know what I mean?''

"Well, I'm happy to see you, no matter why you're here." I threw my arms around him and hugged his skinny shoulders with all my strength. "I just spent all my cash on groceries. How are your finances?"

"I'm loaded, babe."

"Wonderful. Let me go and drop these things off, and then you can take me to a cocktail lounge. I feel expensive."

"You're showing your age, Swede. They don't have 'cocktail lounges' anymore."

"Then how about a greasy hamburger in a dive?"

"I think not, Swede."

"Oh really? Why not, Basillio? Do you have another date?" I was flirting with him, happily.

He didn't reply for a minute. Then he said, "Sweetheart, sit down here for a minute."

I didn't like the sound of that. There was no humor or wit or self-mockery in his voice—in other words, he didn't sound like Basillio.

"Tony, what's wrong? Are you in trouble?"

He sat down on the step, placing the bag between his legs. I sat next to him. A neighbor walked past us with her two ancient dogs. The block fell suddenly silent, and a few beams of light from the streetlamps crisscrossed the gutter ten feet in front of us.

"Tony, what is it? What kind of trouble did you get into up there?"

"It's not my trouble, Swede. It's yours."

"What are you talking about?"

"I called my machine in the City to pick up my messages. There was a call from Detective Rothwax. That's why I'm here. He told me to come and see you."

"Why?"

"He said you might need a friend."

"Why don't you just say it, Tony. Just tell me."

"Yeah, you're right. I'm not handling this very well, am I? I ought to just spit it out."

"Any vulgar metaphor will do, Tony. Just tell me."

He reached over and grasped my hand. I shook it off immediately, my anxiety level at the danger point.

"At about ten-thirty this morning," he started, choosing his words carefully, "your friend Barbara's husband left home to take in some dry cleaning. He came back about an hour later, put his key in the lock, and was blown to bits. He's dead."

Foolishly, I asked, "Tim? You mean Tim?"

"Yes." He seemed almost embarrassed to repeat it. "He's dead."

I stared down into the bag of groceries. I could see the top of the small glass jar of Medaglia d'Oro—the brand of instant espresso that I'm so fond of. I remembered being in the market, holding it in my hand, and thinking that every time I buy it the price seems to have gone up.

17

They sat there watching me, waiting for me to tear out my hair, or weep hysterically—to exhibit some kind of hard-core grief. But I'd done about as much weeping as I was going to do. The tears were all gone, and whatever was left inside me now was not liquid but hard and cold as ice.

Detective Rothwax and Basillio sat side by side on the sofa, casting uneasy glances at me.

"I am quite all right," I said finally.

"You don't look all right," Tony said. "You look pretty devastated, Swede."

"Believe me," I said firmly, "I'll be okay."

"I called Mr. Basillio because . . ." Rothwax muttered, "because . . . well, after our talk, I figured you'd be upset. Seeing as how you were a . . . uh . . . close friend of the . . . deceased."

"We were lovers for a brief time," I said.

Both men tensed, and then each for his own reason looked away from me—Rothwax at the notebook in his hand, Tony down at the preening Bushy, who was sure the visitors were here to admire him.

Finally Rothwax broke the tense silence. "I've got to go soon. I'll just tell you what I know. All of it I got from a guy named Riggins in Manhattan South Homicide. It's his case."

Basillio sat rigidly, not speaking, but meeting

my eyes again. It was a mistake, I realized too late, to have mentioned that Tim and I had been lovers. Even if Basillio might eventually have figured that out for himself. It was just the words that hurt him. He still considered me, in some odd way, his. Not oppressively so, but it was there.

Detective Rothwax went on, jabbing the air with his finger for emphasis. "I want to make it clear that I've got nothing to do with this case. And I'm not about to get involved. I shouldn't even really be giving you this, but . . ."

"Can I offer you some coffee, Detective?" I asked.

"Nothing, thanks," he answered quickly. "Just let me lay out what I got from Riggins. Fill in what you already know from Basillio here. First of all, they say the bomb was a sophisticated device. A pipe bomb, but a real beaut. I mean, *very* powerful. It was triggered by the opening of the door. They haven't determined where on the door—or near it—the bomb was placed. Or when it was placed. There may or may not have been a timer to trigger it."

"What are you saying?" Basillio interjected. "You mean the bomb could have been put on the door days ago? That Roman could have come in and out a dozen times without setting it off—until the timing device went off?"

"Like I said," Rothwax replied, a little irritably, "they don't know yet. It's going to take some time to piece together what's left of the scene. Anyway, Riggins is moving on this thing. He's collecting information on Roman. And I told him about the RETRO printout I did for you. I figured I'd better—wouldn't want him to find out I'd been

digging in Roman's life and tried to keep it from
him.

"As it is, I don't know how much he bought of
the song and dance I ad-libbed, but so far I kept
you out of it." He looked pointedly at me then.
"And I want to *stay* out of it, too. Understand?"

"Yes, of course. Thank you, Detective."

"Last bit of trivia," he said. "Something I
missed when I ran Roman's name through the
computer."

I was prepared to hear that Tim had been an ax-
murderer, a ten-time bigamist, a hit man for the
Mafia—anything.

"Several years ago," Rothwax went on, "he
was involved in a legal dispute over some kind of
design patent. The suit was long and bitter and
nasty. He wound up winning, and the settlement
wiped out the owner of a furniture manufacturing
business. Homicide thinks it's possible the murder
might be tied to that." Rothwax made as if to
stand up then.

"Just a minute," I said. "Haven't you left
something out?"

"Like what?" he asked, suspicious.

"Didn't you tell them that his wife was murdered? That in light of all this, her death couldn't
have been suicide?"

"Hell, no, I didn't!" he barked. "They've got
the facts on his wife's death. What do you think,
I'm gonna pass on that crap about her being a
Catholic? I told you, I am not connected with this
case. And besides, they'll probably question you
sooner or later anyway, since you were more or
less a witness. That'll be your chance to give them
your brilliant theories about everything. And don't

you forget to include your very personal involvement with the gentleman in question."

Basillio bristled and started to speak. But I cut him off before he got the chance. "All right, Detective Rothwax. Thank you for all your help. I understand your position . . . and mine."

I knew that Tony had picked up on my fakery. I had delivered those lines in the style of a deceitful *film noir* siren. Rothwax had helped me in the past and would do so again, I knew, but for now I had to let him withdraw.

I knew that Barbara's death had been planned and executed just as precisely and brutally as Tim's. I knew as well that the setting of my ladylike trap, that crazy trick with the nonexistent letters, had been way off base. It was obvious that I was dealing not with a lovesick matron—we all would have fit that description—but with a cold-blooded murderer. I was now looking for a killer, rather than a crime.

Rothwax was halfway down the stairs when I realized I'd forgotten to ask one important question. I rushed to the landing and shouted down to him: "What happened to Swampy? Was he killed?"

"Who?" His disembodied voice floated up to me.

"The cat who lived in the apartment. Barbara and Tim's cat."

"He's okay. A priest took him in."

"You don't mean . . . Father Baer? Seventy-second Street?"

"Sounds right," he yelled. Then I heard the lobby door close.

I walked back into the apartment. Father Baer! But how? If no one was aware that Barbara even knew the priest, how had Swampy wound up there? My train of thought was interrupted when I caught sight of Basillio, who was aggressively pacing the floor.

I had improvised a spinach omelet. Tony was a little calmer after we'd eaten and come back into the living room with our brandies. We seated ourselves on the couch.

"I told you," I said. "It wasn't an 'affair.' "

"What *do* you call it, then?" He was constantly crossing and uncrossing his legs.

"We went to bed a few times."

"A few times." What does that mean—twice? thrice? forty-one times?"

"That's right," I snapped. "Forty-one times. In one day. A real Roman orgy." I didn't mean to, but I laughed.

"Very funny."

"Oh look, Tony. It just happened. The 'affair,' as you call it, was sudden and short. It was . . . At any rate, it really is no business of yours."

He just stared at me, defying me to leave it at that, and knowing I wouldn't.

"Tony, the thing with him was very . . . what? Unreal. I got completely engulfed in it, I lost myself in it while it lasted."

"You mean the sex was great," he said tonelessly.

"Not that—not *only* that. I mean that, in a strange way, it was just another function of missing Barbara, of trying to retrieve her, *be* her. It was almost another way to mourn her."

"*Ha!* Sleeping with your dead friend's husband is a way to mourn her? That's one of the most interesting grieving rituals I've ever heard of."

"All right, Basillio. I can't justify what I did, and I'm not going to try. Just suffice it to say I came to regret it."

"And what happened? Why did it end?"

"To be honest, I thought I'd discovered that he was sleeping with one of Barbara's other friends—at *least* one other—at the same time."

"God, this is getting stranger and stranger." He got up to refill his glass. "You don't seem to be mourning for him now. You recovered pretty quickly from the news of his death."

"As I said, the whole relationship with him was bizarre, unreal."

Tony continued to stand over by the stereo, lost in his resentment. He seemed to be very far away from me.

"You're not going back to Connecticut tonight, are you?" I asked after a while. "You don't have to, you know. You could stay. . . ."

"Yes," he said curtly. "I am going. Soon." We fell back into silence, until he asked: "You're going to try to show them she was murdered, aren't you? With or without Rothwax. And," he added, "with or without proof."

"Proof! Of course I have proof. There are a hundred threads of proof radiating out from her leap off that ledge. I have a murdered widower. I have reason to believe he was having an affair with one or more of her friends—*before* she died. I have her mysterious sessions with a priest. I have a record of Tim's secret apartment in the Village. To my way of thinking, that's enough proof to push twenty-seven wagonloads of cotton uphill."

He stood there shaking his head. "I have always had great respect for you, Swede," he said. "For your work and your passions, one of which is solving crimes. It's admirable work, and you're very good at it. And one of the reasons you were so good at it is that you were always able to see past the nonsense—all the extraneous stuff—and cut to the quick. You knew how to think, that's what I'm trying to say. You could look at a fact or a person or an event and see something that no one else did. Including me. Something that was there all along.''

I began to thank him but he held his hand up, signaling that I should hear him out first.

''But you have changed, my lovely. Ever since Barbara died, you've been different. And you know what you seem like now, since she died?'' He timed his pause here very nicely. ''Like a loon. Like you could pick up a tennis ball and say it's the sun—and demand that everybody else agree. You run around crazily. You misname everything. You're desperate and jealous and . . . nuts! If you don't watch it, you're going to be doing command performances at the laughing academy.''

I took a few deep breaths before I spoke. I didn't want to say something I might regret forever. What I finally told him was: ''I wouldn't want you to miss your train, Tony. You had better leave now.''

''Swede . . .''

I picked up his grip from the floor and went over to open the door for him. I placed his bag on the landing. ''Safe trip,'' I said, and allowed him to kiss me quickly on the cheek before I came back in and closed the door. Given some time, this would all blow over. It always did.

I took our empty glasses in to the kitchen and tried to rinse out of my mind that ridiculous scene

I'd just played with Basillio. There was so much else to focus on now.

So . . . wasn't it sweet? Kindly Father Baer, Barbara's confessor and coconspirator, had got himself a cat.

18

I spotted the priest's white hair in the small vestibule of the church. He was attaching a notice to the announcement board with a thumbtack. He seemed to be moving limberly enough now, in contrast to the rather cramped way he'd held his body during our first meeting. Perhaps he was an arthritis sufferer.

When he turned to go back into the church I was there, blocking his way.

"Good afternoon, Father Baer. Do you remember me?"

He hesitated, as if trying to decide whether my face was familiar to him. But judging from his own face, mine was not.

"I was here some time ago—to talk to you about my friend Barbara Roman."

He nodded then, his face clouding over. "Yes, yes . . . And now the husband."

"I understand you have taken the Romans' pet."

He was startled that I knew of it. "Why, yes," he said, a trace of hurt in his voice. "Is there something remarkable about that?"

"I wonder if I might see Swampy."

"See him?"

"Yes. Just for a few minutes."

"Very well. Of course. This way."

I followed him through the church and out into

a corridor. He opened a door with a key on his key ring, and then suddenly we were in the parish house. The door opened into the kitchen, and right there, on a large enameled table, yawning and blinking, was Swampy.

"He looks well," I said, and went over to stroke him. "How did you end up with him, Father? You'll have to admit, it's pretty strange that Swampy should be living with you."

I could tell the question ruffled him.

"What do you mean?"

"I mean that when I spoke to you about Barbara, you told me quite distinctly that you didn't know her husband Tim at all."

"And I did not. I never met him, in fact."

I waited for him to explain.

"One of my parishioners is the veterinarian Barbara and her husband used. It was he who told me about this tragedy. He said the cat needed a new home. And since mice are a constant worry to my housekeeper, we were happy to take the cat in. We've had many before."

I took in his story. "May I ask the name of the vet?"

Father Baer's exasperation was beginning to show. "I see no harm in your knowing. But why do you ask all these questions?"

"Habit," I said, still fondling Swampy. "Will you give me his name, please?"

"Rich Doyle," he finally answered. "His office is just down the block—between First and Second Avenue."

"And did Doctor Doyle know about Barbara's having received instruction from you?"

"No, of course not. . . . Well, not that I knew."

"So then the whole sequence of events is just

one big coincidence. Is that correct, Father? A woman with plans to become a Catholic jumps off a terrace. And then someone blows up her husband. Then the priest from whom she was receiving instruction adopts her pet, because a veterinarian who was the cat's veterinarian just happens to be one of that same priest's parishioners. It's a pretty amazing story."

"I don't know what sort of story it is," Baer said, moving toward the door. "I just know that Rich Doyle is my friend, and I was happy to do a favor for him."

The priest's voice was growing more and more distant. Quite clearly, he wanted this interview to come to a close. It hadn't occurred to me before now that he might consider me dangerous.

"Do you remember," I asked, "that discussion we had about her death? When you said it couldn't have been suicide, because of Barbara's strong faith at that time?"

"I don't think you're quoting me correctly."

"Perhaps not exactly. But you *were* skeptical about suicide."

"Yes. I was," he admitted.

"Tell me again, Father, why Barbara didn't reveal her coming conversion to her husband."

"I suppose she didn't want to upset him."

"Why didn't she tell anyone else?"

"I don't know. Maybe she did."

"Have you given instruction in Roman Catholicism to many people who wanted to convert?"

"Over the years, a great many."

"Is it usual for them to keep their instruction secret?"

"I don't think so. Most of them are not secretive. They are proud and happy. Converts are usually very enthusiastic about their decision. They are more devout than other parishioners. Their faith was not inherited but freely chosen as a result of a lot of thought.''

Swampy didn't seem to care for our company anymore. He ambled off and started to inspect some kitchen cabinets.

I looked at Father Baer. I had never truly liked this priest. Or trusted him. Maybe because he talked in such a distracted manner. Or maybe because what he said about Barbara never seemed to have anything to do with her—as I knew her.

"You don't like my visits, do you, Father?'' I asked.

He was too polite to answer. I continued. "You don't believe that I came here only to check up on the cat. Do you? Well, you're probably right. Maybe I also came for conversation, Father. Because she was my friend and I loved her . . . and she was murdered.''

My voice had grown too loud and passionate. I could see the priest wince.

"Yes,'' he said quietly, "I understand your grief.''

"No you don't, Father! Because you believe in a full life after death. Don't you?''

"Of course I do.''

"So my grief is not really comprehensible to you. At the spreading of her ashes, Father, I prayed that some part of her might survive somewhere in some form, and that that part of her would be at peace. But to tell you the truth, I don't believe any part of us survives bodily death. Barbara was wiped out. Exterminated. There is nothing left. She's gone forever.''

My whole body was trembling. I had to get

ahold of myself. This visit to Swampy was getting out of hand.

"Would you like some water?" The priest asked.

"Holy water?" I quipped.

"No. From that sink."

Swampy had returned from his expedition. He looked bored. I wondered if there really were mice in the parish house. I wondered if the parish house used cat-sitting services.

"You think," Father Baer said wearily, "that I had some kind of special relationship with your friend. That I can tell you something that will be of great importance in understanding how or why she died. But I didn't know her well."

"How can that be? You converted her."

"No, I didn't. I gave her instruction. You are way off-base. You seem to have an old-fashioned vision of me as some kind of St. Paul. But Barbara had already made her leap of faith before she contacted me. All I had to do was explain the history and purpose of the sacraments . . . the Church . . . the priesthood. We didn't have any deep discussions on God and Man. Do you understand?"

"I find that very difficult to believe."

"Look. . . . She would ask specific questions about the Mass or the Pope or Thomas Aquinas or Canon Law. But we never really had an intimate philosophical discussion." He paused and stared at Swampy. "Well, maybe once."

"About what?"

"She quoted a saying to me from some obscure Catholic writer. She said it was that particular quote, which she had read as a young woman, which made her conversion inevitable years later."

"What was the phrase?"

"I don't remember exactly. It was something like: 'At any point in time, one half of all creation is being nailed to a cross.' "

I tried to digest it. What a depressing statement!

"Did you talk about it with her, Father?"

"Yes," Father Baer admitted, "we talked about the inevitability of suffering. We also talked about the redemptive power of suffering."

"You mean the one half of creation now on the cross redeems the other half?"

"Yes. And themselves."

Father Baer reached out and pulled Swampy's left ear gently. It was the first overtly kindly gesture I had seen him make toward the cat. Swampy ignored him.

"My grandmother would have liked that saying," I noted.

"Was she Catholic?"

"No. She was nothing, as far as I could tell. She never went to church in her life. At least, not that I remember."

It was odd how once again the mere mention of Barbara had led to memories of my grandmother.

"But you said that the problem of suffering absorbed her?"

"Did I say that? Well, I didn't mean that specifically. My grandmother had a small leather Bible. Red leather. But she never took it out, and never read it unless someone was sick. Animal or human or plant. If I was sick or a neighbor was sick, or a cat or a dog or a milk cow was sick, or a corn planting was infested—out would come that little red Bible."

"Then she prayed for the sick, I take it—for healing."

"No. All she did was read a psalm."

"One psalm?"

"Yes. A single psalm."

"Which one?"

"I don't remember."

"It appears that we *both* have trouble with our memories," Father Baer said, a tiny streak of mockery and self-mockery in his inflection.

"But I do remember a line or two. 'He will not suffer thy foot to be moved.' "

"That's the 121st Psalm. It starts with 'I will lift up mine eyes unto the hills.' "

"Yes. That's the one!" I agreed enthusiastically.

Suddenly I was struck by the bizarre nature of this conversation. Why on earth was I discussing the theology of suffering with this priest? Why was I afraid to ask hard questions? *Real* questions?

"Father Baer. Did Barbara ever discuss her sexual relationship with her husband? Or with other men?"

A rigid mask seemed to slip down over the priest's face. He pulled his hand away from Swampy. It had been entirely the wrong question, I realized, so I tried to shift gears.

"Well, forget that, Father. But do you remember her talking about any of her friends who worked with her in the herb garden?"

He didn't reply.

"Did she mention a Renee Lupo?"

He didn't answer.

"Or Ava Fabrikant? Or Sylvia? Did she mention me? Did she talk about me?"

He didn't answer.

"Are you sure you never saw Swampy, before the cat came here to live?"

That was my last question.

"You will have to excuse me now," he said, showing me the door. "I hope you've been assured that the cat is being well cared for."

I suppose it's a sure sign you're not wanted, when a priest hustles you out the door.

But it *was* all a coincidence—Dr. Doyle confirmed it all. He had been getting coffee at the deli when he noticed the ambulance and the police cars and the bomb squad trucks outside of the apartment building where Tim and Barbara had lived. The super told him about the terrible explosion, and about the cat he was keeping in the basement. Doyle himself had taken Swampy away in his arms.

"Actually," he said, as I sat across from him in his cool office, which smelled vaguely of animal hair and disinfectant, "if Ed hadn't wanted him, I would've kept Swampy myself—or found a good home for him. He's a great cat." Obviously "Ed" was Father Baer.

"Yes," I agreed, "he is a wonderful animal. I think he lies about his royal origins, but he's wonderful nonetheless."

Laughing with delight at my description of Swampy, Richard Doyle—or "Rich," as the priest has called him—broke the pencil he'd been holding. That just made him laugh harder. His joy in living was apparent. I couldn't help thinking that he must be one of the all-time good guys—those men over sixty who retain the very best of childhood until they die. It seemed so right that he should make his living by healing helpless animals.

But then a somber mask slipped down over his face. "It's really very sad, isn't it?" he said.

"First Barb, and then that awful murder of her husband. The whole family's gone now."

"Did you know Tim Roman, too?" I asked.

"No. Well, I think I might have met him once, years ago. But Barbara was more like a friend than a client. She and Swampy. It's so strange to remember that I saw them both only a day before she died."

"You did? You mean she brought Swampy in?"

"Yes. She hadn't made an appointment. They just came in and waited until I had some time."

"And what was the matter with him?"

"I couldn't really tell. He was very agitated, just acting downright manic."

"It's very strange to imagine Swampy manic."

"Yeah, it is. But it's true. He was pacing and making strange sounds and climbing the walls."

"So what did you do?"

"I asked Barb if she'd changed his food recently. Or if he could've eaten part of a plant—they crave chlorophyll sometimes, you know. I even told her that maybe he was catching some of her allergies, since they were so close. But we couldn't come up with anything. I finally gave her a tranquilizer for him."

"What was that about allergies? I didn't know Barbara had any."

"She had a few of them. She was allergic to strawberries, I think, and chocolate and nuts."

"And you think it's possible that Swampy caught—"

"Oh, no. Of course not. I was joking. I don't know what upset him that day, but she called me in the morning and said he was back to his old self."

As I left Dr. Doyle's office and headed downtown, my eye took in the little restaurant—The Healthy Bagel—where I'd gone on that first day of tracing Barbara's neighborhood path. Unfortunately, I had made precious little progress since then.

I checked off some of the things I'd accomplished: slept with a friend's widower; manipulated a New York City policeman and probably compromised him in his professional life; alienated Basillio; behaved rudely to a priest, all but calling him a liar. And there was more—all of it embarrassing. Once again, my deep involvement in the case had kept me from following standard operating procedures. Basillio had said as much, before he'd accused me of being a "loon."

But enough of feeling sorry for myself, I thought. It was time to get back to basics. It was time to return to the scene of the crime—that party. It was time to confess to one and all that I believed Barbara had been pushed to her death by one of her friends. It was time to put away childish things . . . strange loves . . . tales of vengeance. . . . It was time to become a professional. It was time to interrogate suspects. And Renee would come first.

19

Renee Lupo lived in a loft building on Twenty-seventh, just off Eighth Avenue. It was part factory, part residence. Its major distinguishing feature was a remarkably old and well-preserved fire escape, which circled the structure like some huge chastity belt.

I'd been in the apartment only once before, and remembered being struck during that visit by the fact that there were no books to be seen. I knew Renee to be very well read. And she had written several bestselling young adult books about problem girls who had straightened out. I remembered thinking that she must keep her books in the closets.

Her place hadn't changed. It was one enormous room, and a room where everything seemed to have been elevated: the bed, the television, and so on. Even the kitchen was up a little flight of stairs. Everything, that is, but her low-slung neutered cat, Judy, who was black as coal except for one white ear and one white hind leg.

Renee served the coffee on an old wooden milk crate. From the moment she'd opened the door for me, she'd begun crying. Because of Tim Roman, of course. I gave my condolences to her, while trying to imply by my tone that I understood her

grief for Tim had to be different from that of the
others, more intense.

But Renee waved off my sympathy. No, she said,
it wasn't just Tim's death that was making her
weep.

"So much death," she said. "All around us.
I'm almost numb to it. . . . Do you really want to
see why I'm crying, Alice? I'd like to show it to
you. Maybe you'd understand."

I told her that I wanted to see anything she
wished to show me. She reached into the pocket
of her jeans and fished out a crumpled piece of
paper. She pushed it toward me, saying, "Here.
Read it."

The paper contained a handwritten list of book
titles.

*Dubin's Lives. Levels of the Game. Notes of a
Native Son. Artists in Crime. Collected Stories of
Paul Bowles. A Murder of Quality. Brighton
Rock. Let It Come Down. The Good Soldier.
Down There.* Auprès de ma Blonde. *Love in
Amsterdam. Watcher in the Shadows. Love for
Lydia. All Shot Up. The Gallery. The Zoot Suit
Murders. A Bend in the River. Arabian Sands.
Akenfield. Death of an Expert Witness.*

Some of the titles sounded familiar, but most of
them I'd never heard of. I looked up at her in puz-
zlement.

Renee took the list back. "Don't you see? I'm
crying over something I wrote ten years ago. A
stupid list of the books I read while I was sick in
bed over a period of time in 1980. Every one of
those books meant something to me. But now I
don't even recognize most of the titles. I barely

recognize the titles of things *I* wrote. And these days I don't read much of anything outside of gardening manuals. It just all seems so futile. Do you know what I mean?''

If she was saying something about the passing of time—lost time—time invested in ideas or tied to objects that you can't even remember anymore—then, yes, I did understand. But Renee didn't seem to care about my answer. She sat holding her coffee cup, in a kind of trance.

I had to bring her back to the present. After all, I was there with her so that I could start to ask questions I should have asked right after Barbara died. No more elliptical side trips. Straight ahead.

She must have seen the look of determination in my face, because she dried her eyes and sat up in her chair, looking directly at me. ''What did you want to say, Alice?''

''That I believe Barbara was pushed to her death that night. That she did not take her own life. I want to find out who did it.''

She looked at me with a startled face, then a frightened one, as if she were sitting across from a madwoman.

''Oh really, Alice! What are you talking about? It's Tim who was murdered. But not Barbara! It's impossible! Barbara was the sweetest person in the world. Why, even her enemies would have to admit that.''

''I didn't know she had any enemies.''

''Well, you know what I mean. Everyone makes *some* enemies. Barbara was very principled, and very strong. If absolutely everyone loved her, it would demean those of us who truly loved her. Understand?''

''Not really,'' I replied. ''But for now it doesn't

matter. What I need now is your help in reconstructing the night she died. I want you to tell me everything you remember about that night in Ava's apartment—before Barbara was murdered.''

She shot out of her seat, in a rage. "I want you to stop this delusional nonsense right now! Barbara was *not* murdered! She committed suicide for reasons none of us understand. I won't have you going around making these insane charges! If you *need* to believe she was murdered, just so you can give yourself some private-eye kind of business, you are sick!''

Renee's outburst had alerted Judy the cat, who moved with liquid grace toward the sound of her voice. Nothing looks so fearsomely dramatic as a black cat slinking along a white wall. The sight sent a delicious shiver down my spine.

Renee's rage was spent. "I apologize for that fit," she said. "But I just don't think I can take much more." She looked at me grimly and began to play with the big fabric-covered buttons on her tomato-red silk blouse. The color seemed to lend endless highlights to her lively, dark face and satiny hair. She looked like a beautiful gypsy. If Tim had gone after her, it wasn't hard to tell why. But I couldn't help wondering if she knew about Tim and me.

"What is it you want me to remember?" she asked, sounding both tired and somewhat patronizing.

"Anything. Tell me the first memory that comes into your head."

Judy was on the retreat now, ears back, tail lowered. I was smitten with her—love at first sight. I neither loved nor trusted her owner, however.

"First off," Renee said, "I remember talking

to you. I know we were having a discussion, and you had all kinds of things in your hands—coffee cups or something. And then I heard all the cars honking their horns below. And then someone went out to the terrace to check.''

"All right. Go back, a little before that. Barbara was with us, wasn't she?''

"Yes," she agreed. "And then she gave you her cup.''

"No, a brandy glass.''

"Right. A brandy glass. And then she said something about getting some air.''

Renee paused and then said it again: "Something about having to get some air . . ." Then she closed her eyes and shuddered.

"Did you know that she meant she was going out onto the terrace?''

"Of course.''

"Did you see her walk out there?''

"No. Did you?''

I ignored the question. "Did you see anyone else go to the terrace?''

"No. I wasn't looking. I was talking to you.''

"Can you place where the others were at the moment Barbara left to get some air?''

" 'Place' them? Like candlesticks, you mean? No. I told you.''

I decided to change my tone, make the questions a bit less specific. "Tell me something else you recall about the evening. Anything at all.''

Renee was clearing off the milk and coffee cups from the crate. "I'm going to have a glass of wine," she announced. "Would you like some?''

I said I certainly would.

"When I think of that night, and that party," she said a few minutes later, regarding me from above the rim of her red wine, "I think of it—except for the horror of what happened to Barbara, I mean—with great fondness. The lovely food, and the talk, and the friendship. Yes, what I remember about it was the warmth and closeness and the lack of pretense. And I have to hold it in my heart and my memory forever, because we'll never again have such a night."

"You recall the meal?"

"Umm . . . Yes and no. Was it orange duck?— or orange chicken? I remember a wonderful lemon dessert. And how beautiful the table looked when we sat down."

"What were you wearing?"

"I . . . You know, I don't recall."

"And me? What did I have on?"

She just shrugged. I finished my beaujolais and set the glass down on the crate, plumb out of questions. I looked at Judy, who was napping up on the ledge of one of the oversized windows. Renee had not shown me the door, like Father Baer, but I knew this would be my last visit to her loft. We were not destined to be buddies, no matter how the murder investigation turned out.

My eyes rested for a moment on the wine glass I had just abandoned. It was obvious I had not been thorough—there was still some beaujolais left. I picked up the glass, drained it this time to the last drop, and replaced it once again on the crate.

When I straightened up, Renee was standing. She had a strange look on her face, and her finger was pressed against her lips.

It was obvious she was signaling me that I must remain quiet.

Slowly, silently, she moved to a small chest and

opened a drawer. I saw her remove a small silvery object and put it in the palm of one hand.

To be honest, this sudden eruption of strange behavior frightened me. What was the matter with her? What was that object in her hand?

She moved stealthily away from me, toward the far window. So quietly, so smoothly, that it seemed as if I were watching a silent movie. Had she seen an intruder through the window? Did she want me to help?

Suddenly she leaped forward, and I saw the silver object in her hand flash.

Judy, her cat, woke up from her nap on the window ledge, arched her back threateningly, and glared malevolently at Renee—who just stared innocently at the ceiling.

I burst out laughing, finally realizing what had happened. Renee had merely snuck up on her cat in order to clip one of her nails while she was asleep.

When Renee sat back down, she said, smiling: "I can only get one foot at a time, but sooner or later I get all four. The problem is that Judy naps at different times. You have to catch her in a deep nap."

"I really didn't know what you were doing at first. I thought you had gone around the bend."

"You must admit, I move quickly when I have to."

"Yes you do, Renee."

"Maybe" she added, "if you need someone to cover one of your cat-sitting assignments, you can give out my number. I mean, you just saw my proficiency."

"Cat-sitters don't have to cut their charges' nails."

"Oh, Alice! I thought you were a *super* cat-sitter! I thought you did *everything*."

I stared at her. The tone she had used was sarcastic and distinctly unfriendly. Had she resented my questions about the night Barbara was murdered? I didn't acknowledge her comment. It was time for me to go.

But Renee was not finished.

"Why *do* you cat-sit, anyway?" She asked.

"I like cats, and I need the money," I replied.

"I never could understand, Alice, why you aren't rich and famous. I mean, everyone says you're a great actress. Everyone says you're beautiful and talented and dedicated. I mean, what else does a person need?" Her conversation had started to drip with a peculiar kind of hostility and censure.

"Bad attitude," I explained, humorously, trying to defuse the hostility.

"You mean toward the theater in general?"

"Yes."

"But if you've been in the theater for more than twenty years, and you still have a bad attitude, isn't it time you just gave it up?"

"No, Renee. I like the struggle."

"You don't look like one of those women who enjoy pain."

"Who do I look like, Renee?"

She thought for a moment, then declined to continue, switching to a new topic of conversation. She asked: "What about men? Do you also have a bad attitude toward men?"

A wave of enlightenment suddenly hit me. So *that* was it. She was telling me that she had suspicions about Tim and me. Had Tim told her before he died?

"I like men," I replied.

"That's not what Barbara told me."

It was an ugly, dishonest way to try to infuriate me. I knew that Barbara would never betray any confidence. Renee's bitchiness was getting out of control. I was seeing a wholly new side of her, and it made me feel impotent. How could I ask the right questions, if I had no idea what sort of person I was questioning? It was definitely time to go.

"Would you like to hear another random memory?" Renee said as I was leaving. "When all is said and done, my clearest memory of that night is that the peppermint tea was awful."

20

Sylvia and Pauly Graff's apartment on lower Fifth Avenue was cavernous and heavy: old New York, Henry James with a vengeance. Isn't it interesting how one understands the term ''old money'' the very first time one hears it? All my encounters with the real thing had made me decide that it smells a little like furniture polish, and this encounter confirmed that impression.

The furniture was dark and looming. Virginia, the Graffs' cat, was about what I had expected: a bored and imperious seal-point Himalayan.

Sylvia, looking rather distracted and blowsy, greeted me warmly enough. She offered me, oddly enough, hot cocoa—a drink I don't associate with muggy summer afternoons. But I accepted the steaming froth, which was presented in an exquisite Limoge cup and saucer.

Pauly was shambling around the apartment. He had been at the door to greet me as well, but I had the impression that he didn't quite know who I was. I knew he was an alcoholic—a drunk, as Gram succinctly would have put it—but this was the first time I'd seen him in the full flower of drunkenness.

''Tim's murder hit him much harder than Barbara's suicide,'' Sylvia said by way of explanation. Ordinarily I might have just sipped my cocoa and accepted her comment. But my interview with Renee had been so awkward and roundabout that I decided to take the bull by the horns on this one.

So I said immediately, "Sylvia, Barbara was not a suicide. She was murdered. Just as Tim was."

At that moment Pauly banged into an ornate chest and cried out in pain. Sylvia, though she loved him dearly, did not go over to him. Instead she called over her shoulder, "You okay?" We heard him grunt as he refilled his tall glass with rum and orange juice.

Sylvia turned back to me. "Yes," she said archly. "Renee has told me about your sleuthing on that front. But I don't believe a word of it, my dear. And furthermore, I disapprove of this silly behavior just as much as Renee does."

Her patronizing manner quickly brought my temper to the boiling point, and I was tempted to ask her if she thought her own behavior—clawing through the trunk in my bedroom—had been any less silly. But I held my anger in check.

"I am telling you that Barbara was pushed off that terrace, Sylvia. And," I added in a conspiratorial tone, "I am not the only one who believes it. I happen to know that another investigation is being conducted at this very moment."

That bit of mendacity, vague as it was, caught her attention. *What* investigation? she demanded to know. But I was "unable to discuss" that at the moment, I said.

I could hear Pauly's halting footsteps somewhere in the back of the apartment—like those of a heavy blind man groping about.

"Since the eight of us were the only ones present that night, Alice, you are accusing one of us—one of Barbara's dearest friends—of murder."

"That is correct."

"Did *I* push her?" she said huffily. "Or Pauly? And for what reason? It's ridiculous! Someone would have seen the person who did it."

"That's what I'm counting on."

"What do you mean?"

"I mean that someone must have seen something."

"Well, it wasn't I. I saw nothing."

"That can't be literally true, Sylvia. Think— where were you just before it happened?"

"Before what happened? That's just the point, isn't it? No one knew what was happening. There was a lot of noise from the horns below. Someone said it must be a backup on the Drive. Les called out something to Ava. I was with Pauly, and you and Renee were across the room talking about something. And the next thing I knew Ava was screaming."

"Did you see Barbara walk out there onto the terrace?"

"No."

"Did you notice her talking to Renee and me?"

"Maybe—I don't recall."

Pauly was back with us. "Anybody else hungry?" he asked, grinning.

Neither of us answered.

"Come on," he chided. "I'll make us a seven-egg omelet. My specialty."

"Be serious, will you, Pauly?" Sylvia said, barely audible.

He exploded in sudden fury then. "Damn you! I *am* serious! Why do you always try to cut me down? I *am* serious!"

But then, as quickly as it had flared, his anger subsided, and he walked over to Sylvia and picked up her hand and kissed it. The two of us watched him move slowly out of the room, a fresh drink in hand.

"I guess it must be difficult sometimes," I said after he was out of earshot. I was trying to be consoling.

Sylvia flashed me a look that was so vituperative I felt it in my solar plexus. It was worse than the withering glance of a veteran director at a young actor who's decided to improvise. I realized that I'd made the kind of statement that only Barbara could have made meaningful, and only from her would it have been accepted. Compassion was her forte. Coming from my lips the words probably sounded quite false, so perhaps Sylvia had been justified in taking me up.

"If we can continue now . . . ?" I queried. "Please tell me more of what you remember about that evening."

"Friends eating and drinking and talking together," she said.

"Yes. I know that. But that's not quite what I'm after. Tell me some little things. Insignificant, even. Maybe a conversation that you heard."

"I heard a dozen conversations. Everyone was talking, just as we always did when we were together. Maybe the garden was our central concern that night, but only because of the ceremony."

"What ceremony?"

"The tea. The bogus Japanese tea ceremony. We were all worked up over the peppermint tea."

"Oh. I suppose we all were a little carried away," I agreed.

Suddenly Sylvia cocked her head and held up one hand. It put me in mind of Renee's temporarily inexplicable behavior at my last meeting with her.

"You remember something. What is it?" I pressed.

"I was just thinking of something that was said after that anticlimactic tea. Renee said, 'Well, that peppermint was definitely not plucked from the Garden of Love.' " Sylvia smiled ruefully.

I had no idea what she was talking about, and asked her to explain the reference.

"Oh," she said airily, "little bookworm Renee was referring to a poem by William Blake."

At that moment the air seemed to split in two with a hideous crash.

When we reached the kitchen, Pauly was standing near the stove. On the floor next to the table was a large pan, which he had obviously overturned in his effort to fill it with beaten eggs. All around us were scattered broken shells. The room looked like a trampled bird's nest.

"The tobasco sauce threw me," he said, wiping yolk from his fingers. "I was doing just fine until I realized I should have had the tobasco handy before I put the pan . . . the . . . the . . . What did I say, Sylvia—was it seven eggs or eight?"

Ignoring him, Sylvia reached over and snapped off the high flame on the stove top. She then proceeded to wipe up the mess with paper towels. Pauly stared fixedly at her as she worked.

"Sometimes," he said, looking at me and flexing his fingers, "sometimes I have complete control. And then suddenly I'm holding something and it falls right out of my hand. But then, sometimes I have a very delicate touch indeed. Like a clockmaker." Pauly bent down near Sylvia. "I'll help you with that, darling." But she pushed his arm away gently.

"Things just fall . . . just fall away, don't they?" he said to me. "Like Barbara, that beautiful girl. And my friend Tim. You'll have to forgive us," he addressed me very formally now. "You see, we've recently lost two dear friends."

"Yes, Alice," Sylvia said when she stood up. "I'm afraid you *will* have to forgive us just now."

I took my cue and let myself out.

Traffic was very light, so the bus trip home took only twenty minutes.

After making myself a little lunch I rummaged through my overstuffed bookcase. Someday I'd have to sort through all those scripts—I had enough to float a national theater. I found an edition of Brecht's poems that Basillio had given me. An anthology of twentieth-century American poetry. A paperback Wallace Stevens collection I'm sure someone left here years ago. There was even a collection of "choruses" called *Mexico City Blues,* by Jack Kerouac. But nothing by William Blake.

On the way to a cat-tending assignment in Chelsea later in the day, I stopped at the public library on Twenty-third Street.

I had no trouble locating the poem.

The Garden of Love

I went to the Garden of Love,
And saw what I never had seen:
A Chapel was built in the midst,
Where I used to play on the green.

And the gates of this Chapel were shut,
And "Thou shalt not" writ over the door;

So I turn'd to the Garden of Love,
That so many sweet flowers bore;

And I saw it was filled with graves,
And tomb-stones where flowers should be;
And Priests in black gowns were walking their
  rounds,
And binding with briars my joys and desires.

Perhaps "our little bookworm" Renee had cited
this poem as an erudite way of confessing to a
murder? *Collected Poems of William Blake* had not
appeared on that crazy list she'd shown me. I had
no idea what to make of this clue, if it was one.

Maybe I had turned into a loon, as Basillio had
charged. But if that was so, I was in damn good
company. I was mixed up with a group of
murderous, catnip-growing, substance-abusing,
overeducated, peppermint tea-drinking, upper-
middle-class loons.

21

The housekeeper showed me in.

"Ava, what on *earth* is that!?"

I had not been back to the Fabrikant apartment since the night of "the tragedy," as many people chose to refer to it. When I entered the apartment to question Les and Ava, I could see that the terrace doors were roped shut.

She was seated at the long dining room table. Les stood behind her, his arms resting protectively on her shoulders.

"What is what?" she asked from her chair.

"You know very well what," I said. "There's a rope shutting off the terrace."

"I tied it myself," she said, "a few days after Barbara . . . a few days after it happened. I don't ever want to go out there again. In fact, I want to leave this apartment." And with this she turned accusingly to Les, who, apparently, was content to stay.

A few minutes after we'd moved into the living room and I'd taken a seat on the sofa, it dawned on me that I was seated exactly where Barbara had sat as she played with the kittens. In my mind's eye I saw her giggle and point to Renee, who stood listening to someone across the room. But whom?

"Where are Winken, Blinken, and Nod?" I asked Ava.

"Locked in one of the bedrooms," she replied testily. "I'm punishing them."

"What for?"

It was Les who answered. "They somehow got into our bathroom cabinet. Tore open a bag of cotton balls and then knocked over the mouthwash, which shattered. All the cotton balls soaked up the mouthwash, and they played soccer with them all over the house. It was an unholy mess. And our room is going to smell like Listerine for months." He suppressed a laugh. "This, on the heels of the Unfortunate Toilet-Paper Adventure, and the Ruined Negligee Affair, called for a little parental discipline. Right, Ava?"

She made no reply. Ava looked as though she might come apart at any moment. She sat ramrod-straight on her chair, her complexion washed out, her eyeballs like pinpoints.

"Who could believe this would happen to us?" she wailed. "First Barbara, and now Tim. Who could believe it?"

"As far as Tim is concerned," Les said, "maybe it's not so hard to believe."

"Why do you say that?" I asked.

"Well, Tim was kind of a mysterious guy. I can believe he had a lot of skeletons in a closet somewhere. The police have asked us about that lawsuit he was part of years ago. They think someone may have had him killed as revenge. He was very secretive about it at the time—and not just about that. His fortunes seemed to rise and fall periodically. Maybe he was into something shady."

"And do you think Barbara could have been part of something shady too?"

"Never," he said, shaking his head.

Ava turned on me then. "Alice, I think you're the most disloyal, hateful individual I've ever known. How *could* you say something like that about Barbara? Knowing how much she thought of you, cared for you! And how could you be so cruel as to try to make her true friends believe she was murdered? It's vicious, it's . . . *sadistic.*"

"I'm sorry you feel that way, Ava. But Barbara *was* killed. And I see my duty as a true friend as being to help find out who did it. I loved her just as much as you did."

"Stop it!" She covered her ears. "Just stop it!" Then, in a fury, she rushed to the terrace doors and yanked the cord off them.

Les and I both ran after her, in a panic, as if we were afraid that she too might throw herself over the rail. But she stopped short of it, and when we reached her she was looking down at the traffic, sobbing hysterically.

Les put his arms around Ava, and I put mine around each of them. She rejected me at first, but then she succumbed and hugged me tightly. It was a terrible few minutes. I heard the putterings of a traffic helicopter overhead. The strong wind from it sent my hair flying crazily, enwrapping the Fabrikants. We remained out there, embracing, while the traffic drummed steadily below.

Les had led us back inside. That rational, mediating air about him had helped us all to cool down. Les was the type of person one appreciated best in an emergency. And indeed, it was he who

had taken charge of things after Barbara went off
the terrace that night.

I told the Fabrikants about most of the devel-
opments, even the dead ends I'd run into, since
Barbara's death—leaving out, of course, my sexual
liaison with Tim. I was trying to make them acknowledge the probability that Barbara had been
murdered, to make it seem like no more than common sense. But they remained loath to believe that
one of our number could possibly have done
something so terrible. I found it hard to believe
myself, I assured them, but, I said, when I uncovered the killer's motive, the act would no longer
be so impossible to comprehend. At any rate, it
was clear that Ava and Les no longer thought me
sadistic or mad, and I took some comfort from
that fact.

In attempting to cooperate with me, Ava had
enacted a strange pantomime in which she'd
walked about the apartment touching all the places
the guests had sat after dinner that night, as though
the touching alone might call up some memories.
Unhappily, the memories refused to cooperate. I
got fewer hints from Ava than from anyone else
I'd talked to.

Les began his own monologue, taking the pressure off his wife. "I will give you my recollec-
tions, Alice. Ordered not necessarily by sequence
or intensity of experience. Ava and Sylvia spent a
great deal of time preparing the tea. I believe that
once, when I went into the kitchen for ice, they
were in disagreement over the proper number of
minutes for steeping peppermint. There was a toast
before the tea was consumed. The cook had prepared roast duckling, risotto, and green salad.

When it was time to eat, I sat at the head of the table. Ava was on my left, then Tim, then Barbara—no, the other way around—then Barbara, then Tim, then yourself, Alice, then Sylvia and Pauly, with Renee winding up on my right. That's clockwise, you realize. With the serving of dessert and coffee, we repaired to this room. People stood or sat talking in pairs or threes. I had a cigar. I heard what sounded like a major traffic tie-up. I asked Ava to take a look out. She cried out. Everyone rushed over.''

I was not unimpressed. Nonetheless, Les's account, though exhaustive, was of the same basic character as all the other accounts: It was cinematic. Brief descriptions of moments in time: A was here, B was there. C and D talked together. A through H ate together. It wasn't enough. I needed a stage director, not a film director. Someone with his eye on the next movement and the one after that and the one after that—all fluid. On the stage, you can't stop the camera. You don't freeze the frame.

"That was excellent, Les," I commended him. "Now, did you see Barbara at the moment she walked out onto the terrace?"

"Ah, no."

"And you, Ava? I don't suppose you did either?"

"No."

"Why *is* it," I said petulantly, "that no one can actually summon up an image of her going out onto that terrace?"

"Well, why can't *you* do it?" Ava replied sharply. "It's you who *should* remember. She was with you last, by your own admission. You said she handed you her drink and then left to get some air.''

There was no arguing with that. She was right.

"I have a possible explanation," Les said shyly. "It may be because when the terrace doors are wide open, it isn't like a separate entity out there. The terrace is just an extension of the room."

"Well, that's a very interesting concept, Les," I said. "But a fairly abstract one. I'm looking to learn a few more facts."

As I spoke, Ava got up and headed for the kitchen. When she returned she was carrying a box filled with the small teacups we'd used for the peppermint fiasco that night.

"Here's a fact for you, Alice," she said icily. And she flung the whole bundle against the nearest wall. "If we hadn't been so busy congratulating ourselves on that pathetic little crop of peppermint . . . if I hadn't insisted on giving that party . . . if we weren't bored New York sophisticates looking for something to occupy our time . . . Barbara would still be alive."

I tried to tell Ava that that wasn't necessarily true. Remember, I cautioned, that someone had had a motive to kill Barbara. If that person hadn't done it here, they probably would have pulled it off somewhere else. Les may have bought the logic of that, but I couldn't tell about Ava; she was tearing up again when I left.

I did look in on the imprisoned cats before going. They were, respectively, sleeping, frolicking, and chewing at the quilt on a twin bed in one of the guest rooms. Not one of them seemed the least bit sorry for the crimes they had committed.

* * *

From the Fabrikants' apartment I wandered to that park at the foot of East Fifty-seventh Street. It has a sandbox where, I suppose, the wealthier pre-schoolers play, and a few feet away from it there stands a gruesome statue of a wild boar.

I stared out over the uneasy river. To my left was the underside of the Fifty-ninth Street Bridge. Across the water was the Veterans' Hospital, on Roosevelt Island. And if I leaned out a bit, I could see all the East River bridges downtown.

That visit had been a hard one, but not because of Ava's tantrum. For the fact is that even as I empathized with her distress I was making mental notes on how authentic rage and grief are expressed by a grownup—I was still an actress, after all, and couldn't help that distancing thing that clicks into place seemingly at will. No, what had made the visit a trying one was my recognition that all the others . . . *suspects,* for lack of a better word, I was prepared to alienate permanently. But I really would have hated to lose Ava's sweet friendship. I was so happy she didn't hate me anymore.

One queer thread had run through every one of those three awkward, painful sessions with Barbara's friends. They'd all ended with a confession of disappointment in, or hatred for, the peppermint tea we'd drunk. Now, what did that mean? Probably about as much as "The Garden of Love." A garden of love. A tempest in a teapot. I couldn't read those tea leaves now anyway, because the cups had all been smashed.

But I could go to the garden of herbs. Tomorrow morning.

A tanker came into view. It must have had a full

load of oil, for the hull was low in the water. Lord! Were my eyes growing old? The name of the vessel was stenciled in large letters, but I couldn't read them.

22

I awoke with a start at about three in the morning. Another bad dream.

After I'd turned on the light and assured myself that the monsters were not real, I felt better. But I knew I'd have a hard time getting back to sleep. Instead of trying I read for an hour, drinking tea. Peppermint tea, in fact, but not the organic brew that had aroused such rancor in my friends. No, this was the pre-bagged stuff straight from the supermarket.

And it was while I was ineptly sewing missing buttons on a few blouses—pricking myself rather painfully—that I had the thought about "mistakes." I realized how many mistakes all the people who'd been at the peppermint tea party had made in recounting the story of that night.

For instance, I now realized that we'd eaten the duck *before* drinking the tea. Then too, it was Ava, not Les, who had first remarked on the traffic noise.

Everyone had misremembered the facts—*after* I'd told them I thought Barbara had been murdered. Big facts, little facts, everyone had told them a little differently; and everyone had gotten a few things wrong.

I was only waiting for it to be light enough to walk downtown to the herb garden—which was sort of the last terrain I'd left unexplored in this case. Strange that it should be the *last* place I looked. For hadn't the garden been at the very center of my relationship with Barbara?

In fact, that herb garden was central to all our relationships with her. It was just so sad and crazy that we'd all ended up cursing one of our first crops—the peppermint.

I unlocked the gate. It was misty and cool and quiet in the garden. My feet sinking into the dirt a little because of the dew, I stood inside the entrance and tenderly surveyed everything. This might very well be my last visit.

I walked past my catnip patch and over to the peppermint. I removed a plastic bag from my purse and peered into the peppermint to locate the most delectable leaves.

I picked the leaves from four plants and tucked them into the bag. Then I decided to take two more for good measure.

But it was hard getting the buds, the reason being that Ava or Sylvia—whichever was responsibile for this patch—had neglected to do the weeding. Clusters of weeds were beginning to obscure the peppermint.

I ripped those weeds out impatiently and flung them onto the path that ran between all the beds. Then I picked my remaining leaves.

I grabbed my bag and headed out of the garden. But the clump of weeds I'd thrown onto the path bothered my conscience. I knew I should have put it on the compost heap near the gate. So I went back, picked up the litter, and walked with the weeds over to the heap.

They were awfully attractive for weeds. Almost

elegant enough—in their delicate greenness, and with their tiny oval leaves and white creepers—to put into a vase and place on the luncheon table.

I sniffed at them. A pungent, minty odor rose from them. I took another whiff. Well, they were just like peppermint—but so much headier. It was as if they were more pepperminty than the real peppermint.

I could not at that moment have laid claim to a full-blown revelation, but the smallest little ray of light did break through the fog in my brain.

I put the weeds into one of the sacks we used for catnip, and went on my way.

There was a shop on Third Street—Esther's Herbs—that carried our catnip treats. It was almost time for the store to open for the day, But I suddenly remembered that the owners had said they'd soon be going on vacation for a week.

Bad luck. As I stood looking at the hand-lettered "Closed" sign, I spotted someone inside watering plants. I banged on the iron gate and called out until he noticed me.

A young man in a baseball cap, turned backward on his head, came and opened the inner door a crack. "They're closed till next week," he said. "I'm just helping out with the plants."

"I see." I thrust the weeds at him. "Could you possibly identify these?"

"I couldn't identify a 1968 Corvette."

"Beg pardon?"

"Nothing. Sorry, I can't help you. Store's closed."

"Wait!" I called when he tried to shut the door. "Do you happen to know of anyone who could tell me what these are? Any experts on herbs?"

He hesitated. "Just a second. Let me look near

the phone." When he returned a few minutes letter he handed me a business card through the spokes of the gate.

Claude Cervice
HERBAL PRACTITIONER
419 East 9th Street

I thanked the young man profusely, although I knew I had little time. Cervice's building was very far east—past First Avenue.

When I got there, I found that it was three stories of crumbling offices with an empty commercial space on the ground floor. It was difficult to read Cervice's name and office number through the grime and graffiti on the board in the lobby. By stepping close to it and squinting at his name, then taking a few steps back, then forward again, I finally made it out: He was in 3A.

I walked up the three flights. To the left of the door was a bell, over which were the hand-lettered words: RING. WALK IN.

And so I did. The large anteroom was bare, except for several folding chairs leaning against a wall. It looked more like the social room in a church basement than a professional office.

The door to the other room was closed. Music floated out from there. Symphonic music. Then I heard a stentorian voice call out from behind the door: "Sit down!"

Opening one of the metal chairs, I obeyed. My first impression that the room was empty I now realized had been erroneous, for along one wall were piled several cartons with scratchy writing on their sides.

Then the music stopped. The door to the adjoining room swung open and a good-looking, marvelously lanky black man peered at me from the doorway. He was impeccably dressed, but on his feet were a pair of ugly and well-worn tan shoes with leather laces.

"You may come in."

Hundred of books and magazines lay scattered all over—on the chairs, on the desk, on the shelves, on the radiator. A cabinet behind the desk held apothecary jars. And on the wall was an antique map of the Caribbean.

I was then able to put a name to his accent: Haitian. A melodic, French-accented English. A young actor I'd worked with once, who had a keen interest in the occult if not the keenest intelligence, had once confided to me that Haitian people "knew a bunch of strange stuff" that no other people did.

"Sit!" Cervice barked again. But his commands were oddly unthreatening.

I sat in the tattered easy chair across from him.

"Hands!" he said.

"Hands?"

"Show your hands . . . please!"

I stretched them toward him—instinct made me begin to withdraw them when he reached for me— but then I resolutely pushed them forward again.

He examined my left hand minutely, paying special attention to the nails. The same with the right.

"You are diabetic?" he asked, looking at my fingertips.

"No!"

"But consume sweets to excess?"

"No, I do not."

"How much fruit?"

"How much? Well, I enjoy fruit, but I—"

"You will remove your shoes."

I laughed out loud at this. His eyes sparked with anger and he flinched. It dawned on me then what was happening, and who Claude Cervice was. The young man at Esther's had sent me to a doctor.

"Please listen," I said, in an attempt to soothe this insulted gentleman. "I'm not sick. I didn't come here for treatment. I just need some information."

"To give information, I must examine you."

"But you don't understand. I want information on a certain plant. I'll pay for your time."

"How much will you pay?" he said, amused.

"Whatever one of your patients would pay for a visit."

He considered this and then said, "Too much."

"Then how much should I pay?"

"I will think about it."

"But there's no time. Please."

He sat down behind his cluttered desk and began to drum his fingers on the wood. Was he thinking about the price? My urgency didn't seem to bother him at all.

Before I could say another word, a huge orange tabby cat leaped from out of nowhere onto the desk and stood there, staring at me.

"What a beautiful cat!" I exclaimed.

The orange was so bright and so sleek that the cat's body literally seemed to shimmer. I had never seen such a healthy cat.

"He's beautiful," I repeated.

"It's not a 'he,' " the Haitian replied. "Her name is Madame Bovary."

"She looks more like a Rita Hayworth."

"Who is this Rita Hayworth?"

"An old-time movie actress. A redhead of great beauty."

Madame Bovary finished her scrutiny of me, leaped off the desk, and vanished.

"She is the healthiest-looking cat I have ever seen," I told him by way of a compliment.

"Of course she is healthy. She lives in the house of a physician."

"But you are an herbal doctor."

"Yes."

It was very hard for me to believe that cats were treated herbally, by Dr. Cervice or anyone else.

"Do you treat cats also?"

"Yes."

"Using the same herbs that you use to treat humans?"

"Yes."

"But cats are meat-eaters," I said.

"So are humans," he replied.

"Well, I guess it figures. After all, I feed my cats chopped-up greens. And they seem to like it."

"The wild cat," Doctor Cervice said, "kills quickly. And after it kills it rips open the stomach of its prey and devours the half-digested grasses within. So, if one wishes to feed herbs to cats or treat them with herbs, one must rot them first."

"Rot them? How do you do that?"

"Wet the plants and then half bury them. The sun and the earth will rot them."

I wanted to ask more questions but then realized I had strayed far from the reason for my visit. I had to refocus.

"Will you tell me how much you want to look at my plant?"

"Show this plant to me," Doctor Cervice said.

"Let me see it and I will calculate." He seemed to find it all quite funny now.

I pulled the clump out of the bag and laid it on his desk. He sat down behind the desk and put on a pair of spectacles.

"This is what you wish for me to evaluate?"

"Yes. I pulled it up from the garden. I thought it was a weed."

"Ah, well, what is a weed?" he said cryptically, and I thought there was some censure in his voice.

I didn't answer him, of course.

"Tell me: Why are you in such a hurry?"

"It's a long story, Doctor."

"A long story. A short time. Interesting paradox, eh, Miss . . . ?"

"My name is Alice Nestleton."

"And where is this garden you speak of?"

"Downtown."

"Ah, yes?" The term did not seem to have a great deal of meaning for him. "This," he said, picking up the weeds, "is pennyroyal. A member of the mint family."

"So it isn't a weed? It's sort of like peppermint, is that it?"

"Yes. But it is not the American variety. This is true pennyroyal: *mentha pulegium*. It is a perennial. And it has many uses—medicinally."

"Such as?"

"A few are obvious. The name *pulegium* comes from its ability to drive away *pulices*—body lice and fleas. The Greeks and Romans used it for stomach remedies. Also for seasickness. There are hundreds of uses for it."

"Then I could make a tea out of it?"

He smiled. He was very handsome, but for the first time I realized he was not at all young.

"Yes. You can prepare tea from pennyroyal. But you must be careful."

"Careful of what?"

"It would take a few moments to explain it to you. Have you that much time?"

"Please tell me."

Cervice took out a thin cigar from a box on the desktop. He cut off the end with a tiny silver knife and then put the knife in a drawer. He lit the cigar with a large wooden match. He took three deep puffs, then blew the smoke ceilingward. It smelled almost as sweet as pipe tobacco.

Claude Cervice began to explain. As he talked, he kept an eye on the glowing tip of his cigar. I listened with increasing excitement.

23

As Freud used to say—or as people say he used to say—"There's a difference between knowing and *knowing*."

I never really understood what those words mean until the moment I walked out of Claude Cervice's office. As I went down the stairs and onto the street, I knew. The shape was there—large, looming, almost defined. But I didn't really *know*.

It was late afternoon when I returned to my apartment. To say I was excited would be an understatement. I was, to use the current parlance, wired.

Everything I did now was significant. Every move I made was pregnant with the next move. And all my past failures were irrelevant.

I called Detective Rothwax at his home a few minutes after nine that evening.

My invitation to him to meet me in a bar on Twenty-third Street was greeted with a long silence.

Finally he responded, "I'm in my bathrobe."

"It's hard to imagine you in a bathrobe," I said. "But can't you just take it off and put on a pair of pants?"

"Are you going to make sexual advances?"

"No sex, Detective. Just a little alcohol. And conversation. I'll pay the cab fare."

"You're calling Queens, Alice. That's a hefty cab fare."

"Please. I have to talk to you in person."

I could hear him computing the various discomfort factors.

"What bar?"

"It's called Live Bait. It's on the downtown side of Twenty-third, just east of the Flatiron Building. You can't miss it."

"First: You'd be surprised at the things I miss. And second: This had better be good."

I entered Live Bait about ten-thirty. It was a place that had a desperate need to seem funky. Heavy metal music screeched from the speakers overhead. There were strangely-colored baseball caps nailed to the walls here and there. Completely incomprehensible slogans and photographs dangled from the ceiling fixtures. Beautiful but bizarre-looking young waitresses—all of them black, Hispanic, or Asian—floated by, dressed in any way they saw fit. I could tell I was not the typical Live Bait customer.

Detective Rothwax showed up at around eleven. He joined me at the bar. He was very grumpy.

"Thirty-five bucks for the cab," he said when he sat down.

I gave him a twenty and three fives, rolled up. He stuck the money in his pocket and looked around disapprovingly.

"I thought you were too classy for this kind of joint."

"My ex-husband," I retorted, "used to say that I was too classy to live."

"By the way, are you paying for my cab ride home? Or are you putting me up for the night?"

"Take the subway. You carry a gun."

He allowed himself to laugh at that. We had both ordered Bloody Mary's. Rothwax made a face as he sipped his. Then he pushed the drink away, saying, "Let's get to the point of this rendezvous, if there is one."

I folded my hands on the bar. "I know *how*," I said. "I know half of *why*. I don't know *who* yet. But I'm *so* close."

"I hope you're not talking about the guy . . . Roman." I nodded, signaling that I was indeed talking about Tim. "That is an ongoing homicide investigation. You're way out of your league here, lady. We're talking about a professional hit—an explosives expert."

"I know what was involved, Detective."

"And you're *"so"* close to cracking the murder?"

"Murders. Plural. Barbara and Tim were killed by the same person. When I solve one murder I'll solve the other. Here, look." I took out a primitive map of the street where the herb garden was located. I had drawn it with magic marker on a paper bag. Across the street from the garden was an abandoned three-story building. I had labeled it with an R—for Rothwax.

He studied the map, crinkling the edges of it with his fingers. "What the hell is this?" he asked.

"A map. I'm going to need your help."

"For what?"

"To catch the killer, of course! What do you think I mean?"

"Are you kidding with all this crap?"

I went right on. "Today is Tuesday. I'll have the murderer sometime between Thursday night and Friday morning."

"Oh you will, will you?"

"Yes. I will."

"By the way: Who really killed JFK?"

I ignored the comment and pointed at the map.

"I'll be in the garden starting at about nine in the evening on Thursday. I want you to be across the street in that building I've marked on the map. I need you there. It's going to be dangerous, and I'm not overestimating myself on this. I'm frightened."

He knocked the map further away with a swipe of his arm.

"You can't ask me to do this nonsense."

"But I am." I gripped his wrist.

"Then give me something real."

"Like what?"

"A name. A motive. Who's going to be in that garden?"

"But I don't know for sure."

"But you are sure someone will show?"

"Positive. The one who threw Barbara to her death and wired the bomb that killed Tim."

He heaved an exasperated sigh. "And why can't you get your friend Whatsisname to back you up?"

"He's back in Connecticut."

"Send a cab for him."

"Basillio isn't right for this. I want you."

"You flatter me."

"Look, Detective. You're a detective, a cop. Don't you want to catch this person? I can give him—or her—to you."

"How do you know this character is going to

show up between Thursday night and Friday morning?''

"The bait is too powerful to resist."

"Bait! I see. Another one of your so-called traps."

"That's right. Like the one in the park when we worked together at RETRO. That worked well enough, didn't it?" I wasn't about to mention the fiasco of my letter trap.

"Just exactly what is this bait? Catnip?" He enjoyed his joke, never realizing how close to the truth he'd come.

If he went on this way, I knew I'd have to tell him about the Haitian herb doctor and what I'd learned from him. And that would send Rothwax through the roof.

"Detective, may I share with you something my grandmother told me a long time ago?"

"Ah, Christ, do you have to bring that poor old lady into this?"

"She once said to me that most men are cowards. Which is why they're so violent. And it's because they're so violent that they're no good with cows. And a man who can't be trusted with a cow can't be trusted with anything."

He put his head into his hands. "What the hell is the point of that story?"

"My grandmother was wrong. I think you'd be worthless with a cow, but I trust you very much. And I want it to be you waiting across the street from that garden, looking out for me."

"You're playing me like a poker hand," he protested. "Like the audience at a cheap sideshow."

I knew then that he was going to do it. And he knew that I knew.

"But this one is really going to cost you. The price is very steep."

"How much?"

"Don't ever tell me another story about your batty grandmother—may she rest in peace."

"Agreed."

We ordered fresh drinks.

24

It rained that Wednesday, which was good. Rain meant that the little herb gardeners and their life-companions were likely to be at home.

I sat in front of the phone, pencil and large pad in hand. Before you can spring a trap, you have to lay a trap.

The idea was to write the script out on the yellow pad, so that my entire circle of suspects would each hear precisely the same story in precisely the same words from me.

I freely admit it: I'm no writer. The first two efforts at a script were pathetic. The third was serviceable. But the fourth draft hit just the right note, I thought:

The director of the famous Brooklyn Botanic Gardens is coming to our very own little herb garden this Friday morning at 9:00 A.M.—along with a reporter and a photographer. The Brooklyn Botanic Gardens newsletter is going to feature us in one of its issues as being a wonderful community project. Everyone should show up early Friday morning to greet the Director and his staff.

The script was completed. Now I needed an opening salutation. The only one I could think of was rather childish: "I have wonderful news!" I practiced saying that a few times into the dead phone, attempting to sound breathlessly excited as I did so. Then I came up with the more subtle, albeit disingenuous, "You'll never guess who's coming to the herb garden on Friday!"

I placed the calls to the three women. They all seemed excited and happy at the news, which seemed to come like a ray of light on a very dreary day.

Then I decided I should go and talk to someone else.

By persevering, I managed to find a taxi in the downpour. I took it to Seventy-second and Second Avenue. Father Baer was not in his church; he was out ministering to the sick. An assistant—a sexton, I believe—was kind enough to usher me through to the parish house so that I might see Swampy.

He still looked well, if a bit thinner. I tried to gather him up in my arms, but he nimbly evaded me. Then he watched me warily from about ten feet away, his arched body pressed lightly against a table leg. I guess he was chastising me for that vulgar show of affection.

"Forgive me, Swampy," I called to him. "Please forgive me."

The sexton—or whatever his title was—stuck his head in the door just then. I smiled brightly at him, and he left again.

I had come to assure Swampy that everything was going to be all right. That I would soon be naming Barbara's killer. And Tim's. I wanted him to know I understood that no one could ever take Barbara's place in his affections, and surely no one could ever love him as she had, but if there was such a thing as justice in this world he would be able to savor it.

"Understand, Swampy?" I kneeled down near him. "We're not going to let them get away with it, are we, boy?"

He blinked twice. And then stood there and allowed me to stroke him tenderly.

"It's taken a long time, you know. But now everything is falling into place. I just kept getting lost, Swampy. The road kept bending, but I wasn't bending with it."

The stroking he was tolerating, maybe even enjoying. But when I tried to kiss him on the nose he drew the line. Still, he wasn't as unpleasant about it as he might have been.

"Okay. See you again, pal," I said. "I promise. I'm going to bring you lots and lots of goodies."

No more responses from him. He was now staring, the way cats do, at some faroff point in time, or at something I couldn't see. Then, with a flick of his tail, he was off in search of it.

I had to get home, too.

25

I placed myself in the northeast corner of the garden, where we kept the tools. There was no place to sit, so I just stood, doing my impersonation of a rake. I could see the entire garden, the entrance gate, the street, and the derelict building across the way, from which Rothwax was watching me.

What a warm, lovely night it was! Salsa music floated from the windows on up to the cellophane moon. Even the trucks grinding up the avenues seemed muted.

Was I frightened? Not really. I had the funniest sense that I wasn't quite alone, that there, in the dark, Barbara was with me.

"I feel I must confess something to you, Barbara. I went to bed with Tim after you—afterwards. Can you ever forgive me?"

"Oh, nonsense, sweet Alice. It would have happened sooner or later, no matter what. Don't worry about it, dear. He worked his way through half of my graduating class. Anyway, Tim's philandering was so old-fashioned that it bordered on chivalry. At the end of each of his affairs, he was just that much more wonderful to me. It seems the more he played around, the more I adored him."

"Barbara, was Tim doing something illegal?"

"I don't really know, dear. He had his secrets.

And he did love having money. That was one of my few complaints about him."

"What do you think of the garden, Barbara? Or should I use 'Barb,' the way Dr. Doyle does?"

"Isn't Rich a sweetheart? He and Father Ed are such lovely men. Pity Ed has to be celibate. They'd make such a divine couple. . . . Well, anyway, dear, to answer your question: The garden looks wonderful. But is the catnip selling?"

That was Barbara, all right. Hard-nosed common sense wrapped in well-nigh pathological caring.

We talked a while longer—covering the spectrum, as we'd done hundreds of times before. Just as I was asking her if she thought I really was a loon, I became aware of a terrible cramping in my legs.

I looked across the street, thinking of Rothwax and how angry he must be now at having been pressed into this particular service.

It must have been about midnight—the clouds had hidden the moon, and the brooding buildings towered threateningly—when the sense of doubt crept up on me: What if the killer didn't give a damn that a horticultural expert from Brooklyn was coming to inspect the herb beds?

I extirpated the doubt quickly enough—by finding an abandoned planting tub to sit on, relieving the ache in my legs and feet. The night silence was broken only by the occasional shattering bottle or cry in Spanish; or when a car with a very loud stereo idled near the gate. It was an oddly comforting cacophony, for it meant that everything was still normal.

I kept watch, staring into the dark, awake but dreaming at the same time—soft, ingenue dreams.

I even thought I saw Gram coming toward me with a pail in her hand.

Yes, someone else was in the garden. But it wasn't my grandmother.

The intruder was walking calmly toward the peppermint bed.

I scrambled unsteadily to my feet. Suddenly fear had become real. It was on me, all around me.

"Wait!" I yelled.

The figure let out a startled grunt and froze in its tracks. Swinging my flashlight up, I snapped it on.

It was Pauly Graff.

He flung the pail at me. It missed and slammed against the fence behind me. He turned and made for the street.

Rothwax blocked his exit. He shouted at Pauly to stop, that he was a police officer.

Pauly swung his fist and hit Rothwax on the side of the face. The detective staggered, then lashed out with a foot and tripped Pauly, who fell heavily.

I watched in horror as they fought and grappled on the ground, until Pauly screamed his surrender to Rothwax. Rothwax straddled him and handcuffed him behind his back.

"Alice!" I heard Rothwax call out. He was breathing heavily, gasping like a drowning man. Even in the darkness I could see the beads of sweat lathering his face and neck. "Alice! You okay?"

I ran over in answer to the question.

Rothwax and I looked at each other over the body of the fallen intruder. He was breathing easier now. I looked down at Pauly's bloodied face. His eyes were wide open, crazy.

Rothwax looked at me intently. "Listen," he said. "Listen carefully. There's a coffee house on

Seventh Street, just east of Second Avenue. Go there and wait for me. I'm going to book this creep for assaulting an officer.''

I didn't answer him. He shook my arm. "Do you hear me, Alice? Go to the coffee house now! On Seventh Street. Wait for me there, okay?''

I nodded that I understood. He swung open the garden gate for me.

The all-night café was packed. Even at this late hour I had to wait a few minutes for a table. I slid into a seat at the tiny table in the window and ordered a double espresso along with a slab of chocolate cake with rum-spiced whipped cream. My blood seemed to be calling out for that excessive sugar Dr. Cervice had mentioned.

My body was clanging like a church bell.

A lot was clear, but a lot was still opaque.

I was getting old. All the people around me appeared to be children. The young people in the café were talking films and books and love and politics. They were smoking and laughing. And I was still cocooned in my trap.

An hour passed. Still no Rothwax. Poor Sylvia Graff. Poor Barbara. Poor broken Pauly.

Finally Rothwax walked into the café. He looked perturbed. He spotted me and walked quickly over to the table, knocking into several customers. He sat down across from me. The table was really too small.

"We booked him on the assault," he said. "Then I ran a check on him. Jesus, Alice. Do you know who the hell that guy is?''

"I told you, his name's Pauly Graff."

"Wrong. His real name is Ralph Austin Linneus. There're federal warrants outstanding on him for almost twenty years. He was a bomber. A radical. And I mean a dangerous young man. He was a member of one of those left-wing groups like the Weathermen. He's wanted for bombing three upstate air force bases between '69 and '71. He vanished shortly after the last one. No wonder he could rig the thing that blew Tim Roman away so easily. This character knows explosives."

I started to relax. The jangling in my body had stopped. The last piece had fallen into place. The very last piece. That beautiful, simple piece that gave logic and form and truth and continuity to every other piece. The cornerstone had fallen into place.

"What are you grinning at?" Rothwax demanded, picking up my spoon and attacking what was left of my cake.

"I finally know."

"Know what?"

"Everything. Every thing."

"Then why don't you enlighten this poor, dumb, beat-up cop?"

"Get ready for a sad story, Detective. About good women who love bad men too much."

"Soap opera stuff, huh?"

"Not quite. Barbara and Tim Roman had a very happy marriage, even though he was a philanderer. He slept with her friends and God knows who else. But one of those throwaway affairs transformed itself into something very serious. Tim and Sylvia Graff, the wife of the man you arrested, fell absurdly in love. It became so intense, in fact, and so pathologically childish on Sylvia's part, that she actually began to slip Tim illicit packets of catnip from the herb garden to wean their cat's affection away from Barbara to Tim—as if Swampy could be bought.

"To illustrate the intensity of Sylvia's often pathetic middle-aged passion, she wrapped the catnip in her husband's old handkerchief—the one bearing his real initials, RAL. In Sylvia's eyes Tim was the promise of new love, the resurrection of those early years with her husband. Sylvia was a newlywed again. Do you understand, Detective?"

"If *you* understand, Cat Lady, *I* understand."

"I first thought the initials on the handkerchief stood for Renee Lupo. How silly I was. Renee is no sentimentalist."

"Are we getting close to the point?" he asked impatiently, trying to catch the waitress's eye.

"The good part is coming. Relax. First let me tell you about Barbara Roman. She was a beautiful and compassionate woman. People confided in her. People told her things they wouldn't tell anyone else, not even their own family. Everyone confided in her. I did, and Sylvia Graff did. She had told Barbara about Pauly's terrorist past long before Sylvia's affair with Tim.

"Now, Barbara was a very complex person. But she did have a very uncomplicated weakness: She loved Tim to distraction, and she didn't want to lose him. That was compounded by the fact that she was, for her own reasons, taking instruction in Roman Catholicism. Divorce was unthinkable, on many levels.

"So Barbara did what was probably the first mean thing in her life. After she found out that Tim was actually contemplating a divorce to show Sylvia that he was serious about her, Barbara threatened Sylvia. Barbara was going to tell the authorities about Pauly's fugitive status unless Sylvia broke off the affair.

"It is indeterminate whether Tim loved Sylvia for herself or for her money. But Sylvia was deeply in love with him. Yet she also loved and took care of Pauly. Now, it's one thing to fall passionately in love with another man and divorce your husband, another thing to subject that longtime partner to exposure and possible life imprisonment. Sylvia told Pauly about her affair with Tim—and about Barbara's ultimatum.

"They decided to kill Barbara. Their method was ingenious. Sylvia planted pennyroyal in the peppermint bed and substituted it for peppermint in the tea that was brewed the night of the party."

Rothwax held one hand up as if he were a stoplight. "Wait a minute. Slow down. This is *worse* than a soap. It's a Chinese puzzle. What the hell is 'pennyroyal'?"

"A plant. It smells almost exactly like peppermint. But it's used traditionaly as an antidote for seasickness."

"You're losing me here, Alice," Rothwax said. He picked up an empty espresso glass to demonstrate to the waitress what he wanted.

"Pennyroyal, Detective Rothwax, like many herbs, sometimes has a paradoxical effect on the user. Similar in a way to the drug valium. Some people who take valium to calm down end up getting violent—particularly if they've mixed it with alcohol. Pennyroyal helps to balance most people, but for those with certain allergies the effect is just the opposite—it makes them dizzy. The allergies bring on the anomalous effects of pennyroyal, just as alcohol sometimes precipitates the anomalous effects of valium."

"And Barbara had these allergies?"

"Yes. I found that out quite accidentally from the vet Barbara used for her cat Swampy. It was he who found a new home for the cat after Tim was murdered."

"This is starting to get interesting," he said, stirring the espresso the waitress had placed in front of him.

"You see, everyone at the party was given pennyroyal. But only Barbara had that bad reaction to it. Dizzy and nauseated, she wandered unsteadily out onto the terrace. Along comes drunken, bumbling Pauly. A little push. She hurtles to her death."

"Then that's why Graff—or Linneus—showed up at the garden tonight. Right? To get rid of the pennyroyal that was still growing?"

"Exactly. I told everyone that someone from the Brooklyn Botanic Garden was coming to inspect the garden tomorrow." I looked across at his wristwatch. The wee hours of the morning were upon us. "I mean today. Obviously the visitor would have spotted the pennyroyal. Neither Sylvia nor Pauly wanted anyone to know about it, to know that it had been planted among the peppermint. Looking back now, I can see why Sylvia always wanted to take care of the peppermint bed herself. She didn't like to have anyone else butting in."

"Beautiful, Alice, beautiful," he exhaled.

"Like it? Are you impressed?"

"I'm knocked out."

"Thank you. It's nice to get a compliment from a colleague. And you are my colleague—sort of."

"Now tell me: why kill Tim Roman?"

"Because he was clearly unraveling after Barbara's death. Neither Sylvia nor Pauly knew whether Barbara had told Tim about Pauly's past. If he did know, he could not be trusted to remain silent, because he was essentially out of control. So Pauly drew on his old expertise to kill him.''

Rothwax leaned back, seemingly lost in thought. He sipped his coffee absentmindedly.

"I don't want to depress you, Alice," he said, "but while the bomb people will easily be able to make a case against Pauly, I can see no way for Homicide to prove he pushed Barbara off the terrace. No witnesses. No body to autopsy, to see if she indeed swigged pennyroyal. And even if there was a body, and an autopsy showed pennyroyal, it's not a poison. It's just a plant, an herb. Everyone at the party drank it."

"I don't think anyone will have to prove anything, Detective."

"Is that right?" he queried, the old sarcasm back.

"Yes. I think Pauly will confess once you tell him that Sylvia is a suspect in both murders. He'll try to save her."

"What? And she walks?!"

"Maybe. She did brew the tea. She did start the chain of betrayal and death. She knew what was going to happen every step of the way. *But only Pauly murdered.*"

"Sometimes, Cat Lady," Rothwax said with obvious respect and affection, "you have what they used to call in the Academy 'the criminal mind.' "

I turned halfway around in my chair and spoke to the waitress, who had reappeared. "One more piece of chocolate cake, please. Hold the whipped cream. And a large glass of water."

She nodded, looked furtively about, then whispered into my ear: "I saw you in a play at the Seventy-Fourth Street Theater about five years ago. You were just wonderful."

"What the hell was all that about?" Rothwax asked after the young woman had departed.

"She warned me not to order the peppermint tea."

26

Renee Lupo was the first one to call me the following day. She phoned at noon—and woke me. What in God's name was happening? she wanted to know. Pauly had been arrested! And the police were questioning Sylvia. I told her that I didn't know any more than she did. When Ava called twenty minutes later, my responses were just as noncommittal.

But they kept calling. What about the garden? they asked. Yes, what about it? Finish it off with a flourish by harvesting and selling the herbs? Or let them rot in the ground, because too many people associated with the place had already been destroyed? What price catnip?

The calls intensified. I had to get away.

At three in the afternoon I put the cats into their traveling cases and did something I hadn't done in years: rented a car.

A little later I was driving north and east on an ugly old highway, headed for Stratford.

I reached the playhouse around seven. There was no performance that evening, but the doors were open. I walked inside, past the ticket office, and into the theater.

In the typical summer stock arrangement, the stage was a thrust-out, one-set, no-curtain affair. Basillio's work was in full view.

My! What a stunning job he had done for this provincial production of *Julius Casear*.

There were only two elements to the set. The first was a massive white canvas stretched all around the stage—making the entire set, and indeed the entire theater, an emblem of the tents of the Roman Imperial Legions.

The second element, downstage left, was a truly massive pile of yellow ribbon stretched up to the high ceiling, emblematic of the latest patriotic manifestation of imperial America—Operation Desert Storm, in the Gulf.

I felt good looking at it—very good—and very proud of Tony. Basillio had regained his verve, his independence. For him, the stage set was even more important than the script. The set told its own story; it captured the audience in its own way; it could succeed even if all else failed. Bravo, Tony!

Two workmen were cleaning an air-conditioning duct high up on the wall. I yelled up to them: "Do you know where I can find Tony Basillio?"

They told me to try the restaurant called Burke's, he might be there. The whole company hung out there after performances or on their days off.

There was a pay phone outside the theater. I called the home number Basillio had given me. No answer. I decided to try Burke's.

It was, in fact, just a pizza place, but it was cavernous and had a good feel about it. The moment I walked in I heard Tony's voice. That was nice. The only problem was, the voice was very angry. And there were other raised voices breaking into his tirade, equally angry.

I realized that I'd walked into an intense theatrical dispute. Or an intense dispute on theater. Maybe both.

Tony was shouting at a young man with a Prince Valiant haircut, who must have been the director. Tony was saying that he didn't care how many raves the production had gotten, it was boring and intellectually bankrupt—totally without redeeming theatrical value, or any other kind of value. He stuck his finger in front of Prince Valiant's face and said that the play itself was garbage and ought to be banned from all theaters until the twenty-fifth century.

The young man then asked Tony why he didn't go back to New York, if he disliked the show so intensely.

Basillio replied that he was going to give that option some serious consideration.

And then he noticed me.

He didn't move for a minute, not quite believing what he was seeing. Finally he walked over to me. "Swede! How did you get here?"

"In a spiffy little Nissan Sentra. My cats and I were out for a spin, and now we're in need of safe haven for the night."

"You came to the right place," he said, grabbing my elbow and escorting me out.

I drove him to his apartment, retrieved the cat-carriers, and we all went inside. The place was small and rustic, to use the kindest phrase, and full of shaky, scuffed furniture. The kitchen was of 1930s vintage.

Tony was talking a blue streak about how much he hated his present situation: the damn production, the company, the town, the food, the dialect, the audiences, the water, the air (Why the air? I asked him. Was it too clean? But he didn't even hear me.), and a great deal more.

I opened the carriers and let my beasts out. Bushy first, because he hated being inside. Crazy Pancho, on the other hand, looked upon it all as a great vacation, a refuge from his furtive, fugitive existence.

I studied Bushy's reaction to the new surroundings. He sashayed in one direction and then another—stately, slowly, his nose in the air. It was obvious he found these new quarters decidedly beneath him.

Pancho was different. The moment he stepped into the room he went into a crouch, waiting for the bad news.

Basillio was still ranting. He hadn't asked a single question about me or the Roman case. Or what I was really doing up here.

Ordinarily that would have infuriated me. But I soon realized that his lack of interest was exactly what I was looking for right then. I was in no mood to crow about having solved the murders. Nor did I want to brag about the ingenious trap I'd set. And I especially didn't want to discuss Tim Roman—neither the brief affair I'd had with him nor the fact that I still didn't know for sure how many of us he had slept with. Besides, it was almost as though I had expected Tim to vanish sooner or later. He had been one of Barbara's "things," and he would have faded, disappeared, like all her other things—her friends, her cat, her garden. But I had to stop this train of thought. I was getting morbid.

I just wanted it all to vanish, and leave nothing but good memories of Barbara.

". . . and do me a favor, will you?" he was

shouting. "Put those cats of yours back in the car!"

"If those cats go back to the car, Tony, so do I!"

That ended his crazed monologue.

I took advantage of his temporary silence. "There's one other condition for my staying here tonight, Basillio."

"What's that?"

"Do not call me 'Swede'."

His handsome face collapsed in confusion. "What do you mean? What should I call you, Swede?"

"Just for tonight, Tony, call me Alice."

He cocked his head, as if this were only another option to be seriously considered. But that was enough for me. I went to turn down the sheets.

1

Think of the music and costumes and exuberance of *The Nutcracker*! As performed on Christmas Eve by the New York City Ballet at Lincoln Center. Is there any other event which so captures the desperate holiday gaiety of Manhattan?

I doubt it.

But what was I doing there in a first-tier box with five kiddies?

Yes, Five. Count them. Between the ages of six and ten. There was Kathy, Laura, Stephen, Edward, and one whose name may have been Ada or Lara or Sadie.

I was there because in a moment of hubris, I bragged to one of my cat-sitting clients that I could get good tickets to *The Nutcracker* any time I wanted.

Mrs. Timmerman was wide-eyed when I announced that. She asked, "But how?"

"A friend in high places," I replied mysteriously.

Indeed, I did have a friend in high places. Lucia Maury worked in the executive offices of The Lincoln Center for the Performing Arts. Her responsibilities included making travel arrangements for the New York City Ballet when they went on tour. I had known Lucia for more than twenty years.

We had been roommates when we had both arrived in Manhattan—she to dance and I to act. We had kept in touch—one reason being that we shared a passion for Maine Coon cats. Lucia had a wonderful Maine Coon named Splat who passed away about three years ago. Lucia was so distraught that she never obtained another cat. She had been a very fine ballet dancer until she hurt her knee. After joining Lincoln Center in an administrative capacity, she had often offered me tickets, most of which I had refused.

The only flaw in our relationship was that I was profoundly jealous of her while she was dancing. Like many actresses, I have this inferiority complex in relation to ballet dancers. They are so bloody wonderful! They do what we yearn to do and never can.

Anyone who has been backstage just before a ballet starts knows what I mean. The dancers are chatting about everything from boyfriends to shopping trips to the weather. Some stretch. Some put on makeup.

Suddenly the orchestra begins, and a few seconds later the curtain goes up.

One of the dancers, who moments earlier was chewing on a fingernail because she was bored, bursts out onto the stage and executes a series of magnificent leaps and turns.

She stops suddenly downstage, bows luxuriously, and then proceeds to glissade contemptuously about the stage.

In a short span of time the dancer has gone from quiescence to ecstasy, with many stops in between—a disciplined orgy of physical elegance and control.

How could an actress not be jealous of a ballet dancer!

Well, to make a long story short, Mrs. Timmerman was annoying me that day. She kept going on and on about her country house in Dutchess County and how they had decided to stay in Manhattan this Christmas and let the children experience an "urban Christmas." And besides, the cat, Belle, hated the country.

On and on she went, and I had to listen politely. The more she talked, the more she irritated me. So I just casually mentioned that I could get any kind of ballet tickets, including *The Nutcracker* on Christmas Eve. It was my way of showing her that, while I might be a cat-sitter, I had another life—a life that was far superior to hers culturally, despite her wealth.

It was kind of pathetic. I usually don't do those kinds of petty things. But Christmas in New York is difficult, even if one is a Minnesota girl who has lived in Manhattan for more than two decades. And the conversation with Mrs. Timmerman took place only nineteen days before Christmas.

Compounding my stupidity, I offered to take the children as well as obtain the tickets. Everyone was ecstatic except for Belle and me.

So that was why, on Christmas Eve, I was shepherding the kiddies to *The Nutcracker*. That was how I ended up sitting in an opulent box seat at the State Theatre, among all that Noel splendor of light and color and music and fantasy.

Actually, Tchaikovsky was always too much for me. So after the first dazzling scene, I let my mind wander back in time, trying to imagine what the first production of *Nutcracker* in America must have looked like. That took place at the old Metropolitan Opera House in 1940, before I was born. The company was the Ballet Russe de Monte Carlo. The Sugar Plum Fairy was Alicia Markova. The Prince was Andre Eglevsky. When my efforts failed, I just let myself doze off, since my charges were mesmerized by the balletic spectacle.

My doze turned into a gentle fantasy of my two cats, Bushy and Pancho, trying out for roles in an all-feline production of *The Nutcracker.*

I opened my eyes just as, onstage, the Mouse King was about to be extirpated by the heroine.

The door to our box had been pushed open a few inches.

It was Lucia Maury. I hadn't even known she would be at the performance. She hadn't mentioned it. I gestured for her to come in.

She didn't move. She held a finger up to her lips as if signifying that the children shouldn't know she was there. It was very odd.

Then she waved one hand, indicating that I should leave the box.

I did so. The children were too caught up in the ballet to even notice.

The moment I stepped outside the box and closed the door gently behind me, I knew Lucia was in some kind of trouble.

Her thin, angular body was stooped over. She was very pale. The long sleeves of her lovely black dress were pulled up to her elbows, as if she were about to do manual labor.

"Lucia! What's the matter?"

She started to answer and burst into tears. Then,

fighting back the tears, she grabbed my arm and started to pull me along.

I allowed myself to be led. Lounging ushers stared at us. The music from within could be heard only dimly.

She guided me through the mezzanine lobby, past the bar already set up for the coming intermission, and through the glass doors onto the open air balcony.

It was cold. A strong wind was blowing. The city was a blaze of holiday lights. The fountain in the plaza below was spouting magnificently. I could hear the bells from the Salvation Army Santa Clauses on Broadway.

At first I thought we were the only people on that windswept balcony. But then I saw a small knot of people on the western edge, against the building. At least two of them were police officers.

Lucia was beginning to shiver. She stopped about five feet from the gathering.

Suddenly, I could see why they were all there.

Sitting against the building wall was a derelict, without shoes. His eyes were wide open. They were a startling shade of blue.

I was about to remonstrate with Lucia for dragging me out onto a freezing balcony to look at a drunk. After all, there were hundreds of homeless derelicts living around Lincoln Center.

But then I saw something distinctive about this drunk other than his beautiful eyes and the fact that he was shoeless in winter.

There was a hole in his forehead. A small jagged hole. The man was dead. The hole had been made by a bullet.

Lucia increased the pressure of her hand on my arm as if she were falling.

"It's Dobrynin, Alice. Dobrynin!"

Was Lucia mad? "Do you mean Peter Dobrynin?"

"Yes! Yes! Yes! It's him. It's Peter Dobrynin!" She whispered frantically, and her fingers pinched my arm so tightly that I cried out from the pain. One of the policemen turned and stared at me.

Peter Dobrynin? I stared at the shoeless dead man again. How could it be?

Peter Dobrynin had dropped out of the public eye three years ago. The most acclaimed male ballet dancer since Nijinsky had gone into seclusion. There were all kinds of rumors and speculations. He had gone into a drug rehab clinic. He had entered a monastery in Vermont. He had been admitted into a mental hospital. No one knew for sure.

But what an impact this one-time student of the Kirov Ballet had made on the dance world before he dropped out.

He was bigger and more powerful and more dramatic than Baryshnikov, more technically proficient and more musical than Nureyev. His roles in *Giselle* and *Firebird* and *Petrouchka* had made him the new hero of the American ballet.

And Dobrynin was as flamboyant offstage as he was onstage—lover, brawler, lunatic, junkie, drunk, frequenter of jet-set parties as well as funky Harlem discos. He was always out of control.

Lucia started to pull me away. But I fought to stay, to keep staring at the corpse. Had this dreadful wreck of a man really once been the golden dancer, Dobrynin?

The wind began to whip across the open balcony, making me shudder. After all, it was Christmastime in New York.

Lydia Adamson is the pseudonym of
a well-known mystery writer.